# MATCH WITS WITH TRIXIE!

Trixie Belden has a thrilling challenge for you!

Match wits with Trixie as she solves some baffling mysteries and grapples with some perplexing quizzes.

Test your powers of observation with ingenious cartoon mysteries. Spot the hidden clue! It's in there, somewhere—but you have to be sharp to see it!

Minute mysteries challenge your deductive skills. Unravel the clues and find the villain. You have to be quick, though—or the villain might escape!

Dozens of quizzes on all sorts of subjects mystify your mind. There are even cryptic quizzes in code for you to decipher!

And here's an extra-special bonus—a Trixie Belden short story for you to enjoy!

So sharpen your pencils and your wits and join America's favorite girl detective for mystery, adventure—and fun!

# Trixie Belden
## MYSTERY-QUIZ BOOK Number 2

BY KATHRYN KENNY
with
Joan Bowden
Mary Carey
Eileen Daly
D.J. Herda
Betty Ren Wright
and others

•

Illustrated by
Jack Wacker and Erv Gnat

cover by Jim Wagner

•

GOLDEN PRESS
Western Publishing Company, Inc.
Racine, Wisconsin

# CONTENTS

# WHAT DO YOU KNOW ABOUT FIGHTING CRIME?

"What **do** I know about fighting crime?" Trixie asked herself as she began to answer the following quiz. "Well, for one thing, I know that I don't know as much about it as I thought I did. Hmmm. . . ."

1. It is now believed that no two voices are identical, just as no two fingerprints are alike. True or false?

2. There are no international criminal laws. True or false?

3. FBI agents are sometimes called G-men. What does the G stand for?

4. The voice makes shape patterns, called voiceprints. Can these be changed by disguising the voice?

5. Is it possible for an amateur to make a plaster cast of a footprint in snow?

6. Dactyloscopy, a common and useful police science, is really just establishing identity by _____ .

7. A polygraph, or lie detector, gives one clear signal when an untruth is told. True or false?

8. What is INTERPOL?

9. INTERPOL headquarters are in
   a. France.      b. England.      c. New York.

10. What are three rights guaranteed a person by the "Miranda Warning"?

# THE CASE OF THE DOMINANT DAME

Trixie and Honey are trying to figure out who the leader of a notorious gang of female burglars is. They have four suspects: Gorgeous Gladys, Second-Story Cynthia, Larcenous Lil, and Freda the Filcher. They have these clues:

1. Two of the suspects are blond, and one is brunet.

2. The red-haired suspect has green eyes, and two of the others have brown eyes.

3. Lil has the same hair color that Gladys has, and her eyes are the same color as Freda's.

4. The leader has blue eyes.

Who is the leader of the gang?

HINT: A good way to solve this kind of quiz is to chart all the clues.

Example:  <u>blond</u>  <u>blond</u>  <u>brunet</u>  <u>redhead</u>
             Lil      Gladys


# THE CASE OF
# THE UNCERTAIN SEATING

Trixie, Mart, Brian, Honey, Jim, and Di go into town in the Bob-White station wagon to see a movie. Two of the girls sit in the front seat with one of the boys, and the third girl is in the backseat with two boys. Trixie sits next to Jim, and Di has Mart on her left and another person on her right. Jim and Brian are the only ones in the group who have driver's licenses. Who is driving, and where does each of the other passengers sit?

# MUSICAL MYSTERY

Trixie and Honey were riffling through the newspaper, when an ad in the "Musical Instruments, Buy and Sell" section caught their attention. It read:

For sale: Have got to sell my grand piano. Although I've had it since my first lesson, the bank's about to claim it along with all my other goods unless I can sell it. Will accept best offer. I can't deliver, but it can be picked up anytime.

The next day, another unusual ad appeared, which read:

Am trying to corner the American market on instruments with strings tuned a sixth or fifth lower than normal. Will search every avenue and alley. Will leave no stone unturned. Will pay any fair price—no need to drive a hard bargain. Must have replies by Friday. Bonus paid if at least four instruments available at same address.

Something about these ads aroused the mystery-solving instincts of both girls, and they realized that the ads were really a code of some sort. Sure enough, the girls broke the code, thus playing a major role in nabbing some local bank robbers. How did they do it?

# REDHEADED THIEF

When Trixie heard Honey's news, she couldn't believe it. Someone had broken into the principal's office and stolen some money—and redheaded Jim Frayne was suspected of the crime!

"Jim wouldn't steal anything!" Trixie sputtered. "None of the Bob-Whites would!"

When they reached the school office, Honey clutched Trixie's arm hard. Two boys with flushed faces sat waiting outside the principal's door. One of the boys was Jim! The other was redheaded Larry Gibson.

"There's nothing you can do, Trix," Jim said miserably. "Mr. Stratton asked us both to wait here while he questions the custodian again. I don't know why—he's told his story twice already. He saw a redheaded boy run out of this office at seven o'clock this morning. He's certain it was either Larry or me."

"But you weren't even here at seven o'clock, Jim," Honey cried.

Jim shook his head. "Yes, I was. I came early to study for a math test. But I wasn't anywhere near this office."

"I wasn't here," Larry Gibson declared. "I've already told Mr. Stratton that I was at home when the theft took place."

"Can you prove it?" Trixie asked him.

"I told Mr. Stratton that I can't prove anything," Larry said, "but since then, I've been thinking. And I think I can prove my story, after all. You see, at seven o'clock this morning, my Aunt Mary called me from California. She used to live here in Sleepyside, and she still likes to hear all the latest news of downstate New York."

"Are you sure she called at seven o'clock?" Honey asked suspiciously.

"I'm positive," Larry replied smugly. "As I picked up the phone, I plainly heard her old grandfather clock chime seven times."

"Well, I'm positive, too," Honey whispered to Trixie. "I'm positive he's lying. Larry must have stolen the money. Am I right?"

"Positively!" Trixie whispered back, grinning with relief. "And when Mr. Stratton hears his story, he'll be positive, too."

How did Larry give himself away?

# THE
# KIDNAPPED
# CAMPER

294

> WE WERE GOING TO GET UP EARLY TO FISH, BUT WHILE WE WERE STILL SLEEPING, AN ARMED MAN JUMPED US. HE SAID HE'D KILL HARRY IF I TRIED TO STOP HIM, THEN HE FORCED HARRY TO GO WITH HIM.

④

> HOW LONG AGO DID IT HAPPEN?

> WHAT DID YOU DO?

> WHERE DID THEY GO?

> ABOUT FIFTEEN MINUTES AGO, I GUESS. I WAS TOO SCARED TO DO ANYTHING AT FIRST. THEN I REMEMBERED SEEING YOUR FIRE LAST NIGHT, SO I RAN FOR HELP. THEY WENT THAT WAY.

⑤

> GLEEPS! THE KIDNAPPER WANTS A HALF A MILLION DOLLARS!

> HE WON'T GET IT! HE MADE A MISTAKE WHEN HE TRIED TO KIDNAP HIS OWN CAMPING PARTNER!

⑥

**HOW DID TRIXIE KNOW THAT THE MAN HIMSELF WAS THE KIDNAPPER?**

15

# PIRATES AND PIRATE TREASURE

Trixie came bounding down the library steps and rushed over to Brian, who was waiting for her in his jalopy. "Just wait until I tell you all of the fascinating things I found out about pirates and pirate treasure!" she exclaimed, scrambling into the front seat.

"Trixie, you're getting to be a walking fact book on pirates and pirate treasure," Brian said.

"It's because I've been writing a paper about them for school. Here's a quiz I made up about some of it."

1. A pirate perch is a
   a.fish.　　　b.gangplank.　　　c.lookout roost.

2. Bermuda waters are called the "graveyard of ships" because the number of sunken vessels there is about
   a.1,000.　　　b.6,250.　　　c.600.

3. It is claimed that pirate treasure is buried all along the Gulf Coast from Florida to Texas. True or false?

4. Were buccaneers' doubloons bell-bottomed or straight-legged?

5. Why were others filled with even greater fear when pirates flew a red flag instead of the usual black flag?

6. The "Lost Loot of Lima," the treasure of one pirate, is supposed to be worth
   a. $700,000.     b. $98,000.     c. $65,000,000.

7. An author drew a map of an imaginary island and then wrote a story about it for his stepson. Name this book, which became one of the best known adventure tales about pirates.

8. What famous English navigator and explorer also committed acts of piracy?

9. Two unusual pirates managed to fight side by side with buccaneers who would never have allowed either aboard had they known a certain fact about them—a fact that most pirates feared would bring ill fortune to any ship such persons sailed on! Who were the pirates, and how were they unusual?

10. Treasure map codes.

Some pirates used their own personal system for coding their hiding places. Many pirates, however, used common symbols. Here are a few of the common markings. Can you tell what each one means?

# RODEO CLOWN

The Arizona sun was warm and pleasant as the Bob-Whites sat near the corral fence. They were watching an exciting rodeo.

Trixie's blue eyes were shining. "We've seen the barrel racing and the calf roping. What's next?"

"It's bull riding," Dan answered, "but I don't know much about it. Do you, Mart?"

"It's simple," Mart drawled. "The noble vaqueros bestride the spinal zones of the bovine vertebrates, and the irritated quadrupeds then strive mightily to disenthrone them."

"Whatever you said sounds dangerous!" Di declared. "What happens if a cowboy falls and the bull charges at him?"

A young cowboy wearing a bright red shirt heard her question. "Howdy," he said. "My name is Hank Summers. The fact is, them thar bull-ridin' fellers can be mighty helpless without the clowns to help them."

Di shaded her eyes. "I don't see any clowns. Where are they?"

"Oh, I don't mean your circus-type clowns," Hank answered, chuckling. "A rodeo clown wears a bright-colored shirt like mine. And if a cowboy is bucked off the bull's back—why, ma'am, the clown is there to distract the bull's attention. Yep, those bulls really like bright colors. All us bullfighters know that."

Di looked at him admiringly. "Are you one of the clowns?" she asked.

Hank chuckled. "I shore am, ma'am," he said. "As a matter of fact, I've jest been hired. When I told the corral boss how experienced I was at this bull-clownin' business, he hired me on the spot."

Hank turned and hurried away.

Puzzled, Trixie stared after him. Then all at once, she jumped up and cried, "We've got to stop him! He could get killed if he goes into the ring! He's no more used to handling bulls than we are!"

Why was Trixie so sure Hank was a phony?

# LOST LETTERS

Trixie's best friend, Honey, found some slips of paper in an old geography book. The name of an American city and its state had been printed on each piece of paper, but the sides of each paper had been torn off.

Trixie and Honey were able to add the correct letters before and after those on the slips of paper to spell out all the cities and their states. Can you do as well as the schoolgirl shamuses?

## HARDHEADS AND SUCKERS

Trixie has a special feeling for Jim. She thought he felt the same way about her—so when he passed her this note, she was crushed. When Trixie stopped to think about it, though, she realized Jim wasn't calling her nasty names, after all—he was helping her with an assignment! She turned and gave him the grateful smile he was hoping for. What class was the assignment for, and what was the note all about?

| | |
|---|---|
| Hardhead | Sucker |
| Mossbunker | Spottail Shiner |
| Brown Bullhead | Menhaden |
| Mummichog | Crappie |
| Jack Crevalle | Fourspine Stickleback |
| Tomcod | Johnny Darter |

# INSCRUTABLE BEDTIME STORIES

Trixie said she was sure she knew all the bedtime stories ever written after reading to Bobby so often. Mart bet her a week's worth of dishwashing that she couldn't name five stories he would describe. Trixie had a hard time with Mart's circuitous language, but she finally named them all—and Mart headed for the kitchen sink. Can you decipher Mart's devious descriptions as well as Trixie did?

1. An inappreciable ingenue, swathed in a rufous pelisse with capuche, perambulates for a sojourn with a certain canescent relative and experiences an appalling encounter with an edacious predator.

2. A pauperized hobbledehoy chaffers his mater's bovine for a modicum of legumes, gammons a titan, and eventually finds himself in circumstances unmitigatedly affluent.

3. A towheaded gamine gormandizes farina in abundance, bestraddles upholstery freely, and rests in the arms of Morpheus without stint, thereby failing to achieve a bosom comity with a musquaw ménage.

4. Whilst vagabondizing within a coppice, the bantlings of a common progenitor are well-nigh metamorphosed into the entrée for a senescent sorceress.

5. Porcine triplets contend in a dissension involving fabrication of places of lodgment, with the victor acquiring a caldron replete with lupine ragout.

# THE SUSPICIOUS PROFESSOR

YOU WERE RIGHT, TRIX— THE PROFESSOR'S GOING TO HIS LAB.

IT'S THE ONLY PLACE IN TOWN WHERE THAT KIND OF BOMB CAN BE MADE.

AND PROFESSOR DI GRAVIO IS THE ONLY ONE IN TOWN WHO KNOWS HOW TO MAKE ONE!

WE'D LIKE TO ASK YOU SOME QUESTIONS, SIR.

YES, WE THINK YOU MAY KNOW SOMETHING ABOUT THE BOMB THAT EXPLODED LAST NIGHT.

**5**

I'M A SCIENTIST. WHY WOULD I KNOW ANYTHING ABOUT A BANK ROBBERY?

**6**

THE POLICE SAY THAT SOMEONE IN TOWN WAS INVOLVED.

ARE YOU ACCUSING ME?

**7**

NO, SIR, BUT THE BOMB MUST HAVE BEEN MADE HERE.

NONSENSE! I HAVE THE ONLY KEY TO THIS LAB, AND I HAVEN'T BEEN HERE FOR A WEEK. AND YOU CAN SEE THAT NOBODY'S BROKEN IN.

**8**

EITHER SOMEONE ELSE HAS A KEY, OR **YOU'VE** BEEN HERE, PROFESSOR. BRIAN, PLEASE CALL SERGEANT MOLINSON AND ASK HIM TO COME HERE.

**9**

# HOW DID TRIXIE KNOW THE PROFESSOR WAS LYING?

23

# LONG-LOST GRANDSON

Trixie and Honey looked at the handsome young man who stood in the Wheelers' living room.

"My name is John Baker," he told Honey, "and I need your father's help. I want him to tell my grandmother that I'm her long-lost grandson. I know she'll believe him."

Honey stared. "I don't understand."

Trixie didn't understand either. "Doesn't your grandmother know who you are?" she asked.

"She's never seen me before. I was born in Italy and lived there until a couple of years ago," the young man explained. "Then my parents both died, and I went off to see the world. Now I've come to the United States to be with her. But someone else is also claiming to be her long-lost grandson!"

Honey still looked perplexed. "But how can my father help you?" she asked.

"Mr. Wheeler can tell my grandmother that I'm the real John Baker," the young man said.

24

"I've been told that he knew my parents well, and I know I look very much like my father."

Trixie frowned. "But you must have some papers—something to prove your identity."

The young man shook his head. "I lost all my papers in Australia," he said ruefully. "It happened on New Year's Day, and it was my own fault. It was very mild last winter, so I decided to explore the bush country. All my papers were in the pocket of my leather jacket. When I went to bed, I took it off. It was gone the next morning. All I can figure out is that some dingoes took it. I'd heard them earlier, but I never thought they'd get that near a fire."

"What an experience!" Honey said. "But don't worry. I'm sure my father can help expose the phony grandson."

"If he can't, I can!" Trixie whispered in Honey's ear. "We're looking right at him! I'm sure this guy is nothing but a fortune hunter who happens to look like the Baker family."

How did Trixie know that?

# BATTER UP!

When Mart bragged too long about his baseball knowledge, Trixie sneaked down to the library to make up this quiz. The questions aren't really that difficult, but Mart was stumped more than once.

1. During the regular season, how many umpires are usually on the field?

   a. six  b. four  c. two  d. nine

2. What position did Babe Ruth play before he became a regular outfielder?

   a. catcher  b. pitcher
   c. shortstop  d. third base

3. Baseball owes its origin to the English game of

   a. Rounders.  b. Cricket.
   c. Roque.  d. Paddleball.

4. When professional baseball first became popular, place hitting was the rule. What player was first to establish home runs as a common (if special) event in the game?

   a. Babe Ruth  b. Lou Gehrig
   c. Rogers Hornsby  d. Stan Musial

5. Home plate is as long as it is wide, which is

   a. fifteen inches.  b. twelve inches.
   c. eighteen inches.  d. seventeen inches.

6. What team won an unprecedented eight World Series in twelve years?
   a. Boston Red Sox    b. Brooklyn Dodgers
   c. Chicago Cubs       d. New York Yankees

7. The distance between bases on a diamond is
   a. 85 feet.           b. 60 feet 6 inches.
   c. 90 feet.           d. 35 feet 9 inches.

8. If the World Series were being played by this team in their home stadium, all the games would be played in the daytime. The team is the
   a. Kansas City Royals.   b. Chicago Cubs.
   c. Minnesota Twins.       d. Oakland A's.

9. What piece of equipment **doesn't** a catcher wear?
   a. shin guards       b. chest protector
   c. shoulder pads     d. face mask

10. In baseball, the initials **ERA** stand for
    a. Excellent Running Advance.
    b. Estimated Run Average.
    c. Earned Run Average.
    d. Exceptional Running Award.

---

# QUICKIE QUIZ #1

At Christmastime, Bobby Belden coaxes everyone he can to read **The Night Before Christmas** to him. Like many six-year-olds, Bobby has it almost memorized—but he can never quite remember the names of all eight reindeer. Can you name them? What was the author's name, and what did **he** title his poem?

# BAFFLERS

Knowing how well Trixie likes to solve mysteries, Jim prepared these bafflers for her. They didn't baffle Trixie for long. Do they baffle *you?*

### 1. Who did what?

For ages they said, "Can't be done!"—
Even after the feat was begun.
  Then N. A. A. came
  And accomplished the same,
With a small step he called number one.

### 2. What am I?

I once was called "Lizzie" by some.
With the aid of a strong arm, I'd hum.
  Then I'd shimmy and shake,
  Put a cloud in my wake,
And be off to—who knows? Here we come!

### 3. What am I? What recent record did I make?

I carried three passengers far—
Not by bus, plane, or boat, train, or car;
  And with no motor's aid,
  A record I made
In a way thought by some quite bizarre.

# COUNTERFEIT ART

"Look, Di!" Honey pointed to a drawing hanging on the wall of the Sleepyside Museum. "There's that beautiful line drawing we saw at the special display at school last week."

"Oh, Honey, that's a fake!" Di gasped. "Look. Here's a photograph I took of the real drawing, and that isn't it at all! Let's get Trixie and tell the curator, quick!"

What things did Di notice that convinced her that the museum art was counterfeit?

# LITTLE BOYS GONE!

Trixie's heart skipped a beat when she heard Di's frantic voice on the other end of the line.

"Trixie!" Di wailed. "You have to come over here right away! Your brother Bobby has mysteriously disappeared! And—and my twin brothers, Larry and Terry, have disappeared with him! They've all vanished into thin air!"

Trixie's thoughts were racing as she went out into the cold of the winter day. The snow, which had fallen just a few minutes before, crunched under her heels as she hurried toward the Lynch mansion.

"Now calm down and tell me all about it," Trixie said a few minutes later to a tearful Di. "Start at the beginning."

"Well, I was playing with the boys in our family room," Di began, her voice still quivering. "You know how much I like to baby-sit."

Trixie nodded. "Go on, Di," she prodded. "What happened then?"

"They kept wanting to go to the paddock to visit Sunny," Di continued, a little calmer. "I wouldn't let them go because I knew it was about to snow. Then the phone rang. It was Honey. I guess we talked longer than I thought. When I got back, it was snowing hard, and the room was empty. One of the maids said that the boys had gone to the paddock, after all."

"Then they must still be there," Trixie said. "It shouldn't be hard to find them in a big open area like that."

"But that's just it!" Di moaned. "They're not there. They've vanished! Look—you can see for yourself right out this window!"

Three sets of footprints showed clearly in the newly fallen snow. The deep, rounded toe marks could only have been made by three pairs of small sneakers. The footprints led directly from the side door of the house to the paddock, then stopped. There was no other sign of the three little boys at all! Only Sunny, Di's palomino, stood gazing back at Trixie.

Di clutched Trixie's arm. "What'll we do?" she wailed. "Shall I call the police?"

Trixie looked down at her own feet. She looked at the footprints. Then she shouted with laughter. "Oh, Di!" she gasped at last. "I can guess exactly where they are!"

Where were the three missing boys?

# LOSERS—AND WINNERS

"If you'd lost two hundred and fifty horse races and had *never* ridden a winning horse, would you try again?" Regan asked Dan as they waited at the stable for their friends.

"Two hundred and fifty! I don't know. I'd be pretty discouraged," Dan answered. "Why? Did that happen to somebody?"

"Yup. It's in a quiz I found for Trixie. It's interesting to know what happened to the jockey after all those losses. Here—look at it if you like." Regan handed the quiz to Dan.

1. Which of the following famous jockeys rode his first winning horse after losing two hundred and fifty races—and then went on to set a record for stake races **won?**
   a. Eddie Arcaro    b. Steve Brooks    c. Willie Shoemaker

2. A fellow named Kitchner is said to be history's lightest jockey. What did he weigh?
   a. 59 pounds    b. 49 pounds    c. 79 pounds

3. Is every Thoroughbred racehorse **in the world** a direct descendant of one of three horses imported to England?

4. In a **maiden race,** the horses
   a. are all females.    b. have never won a race before.
                c. have never raced before.

5. What news? What news!

   While running a two-mile steeplechase, one horse would not try the fourth jump. His rider, thinking all was lost, rode back to the paddock. Then, upon hearing certain news, he returned to the race—and won, even though his racing time was almost triple the normal time for the steeplechase! What was the news that he heard?

# WHAT A STATE!

"Briefly speaking," Jim said to Trixie, "can you write out these states for me?"

"Oh., I Kan. Penn. them all!" Trixie told him.

1. Noah would have felt right at home in this state.

2. If you're looking for a bulky state, here it is.

3. A stately number? Not if a little misspelling bothers you.

4. A stated fact? Investigate before you start mining!

5. Doctors will agree that it's a professional state.

6. Relatively speaking, we've each had one of these.

7. This one-word command means **We must remove the dirt!**

8. A sad state of affairs for a player at bat.

9. Most of us hope not to be in this state, but we usually are at one time or another.

10. You never say that I am this, and I would never call you this, but we both use this in speaking of ourselves.

# TONGUE TANGLERS

Di sometimes gets the meaning of her words mixed up, but she can say all of these tongue tanglers better and faster than the other Bob-Whites. How many times can you say each one correctly in one minute?

1. yellow Yo-Yo

2. The sinking ship sank.

3. sixty-six sick chicks

4. literally literary literature

5. The wristwatch shop shuts soon.

6. raw walrus

# THE

# MISSING

# FOOTPRINTS

DIDN'T OUR ESTEEMED MATERNAL PROGENITOR REQUEST THAT WE EFFECT THE TRANSFERENCE OF HER DIGITAL CHRONOMETER TO THE PROPRIETOR OF THIS EMPORIUM FOR REVIVIFICATION?

CAN WE DO WHATEVER YOU SAID LATER, MART? RIGHT NOW WE HAVE TO DROP OFF MOM'S WATCH TO BE FIXED HERE.

HELP! POLICE! I'VE BEEN ROBBED!

HE WAS TALL AND THIN AND HAD A WOMAN'S STOCKING OVER HIS FACE. HE WORE GLOVES—AND HE HAD A GUN! IT WAS TERRIBLE, I TELL YOU!

34

IT HAPPENED AN HOUR AGO. I'D JUST PUT THE KETTLE ON THE FIRE FOR LUNCH WHEN HE CAME IN. HE GAGGED ME AND TIED MY HANDS BEHIND ME AND DRAGGED ME INTO THE CLOSET!

5

THERE'S THE ROPE HE TIED ME WITH. HE GAGGED ME WITH ONE OF MY POLISHING CLOTHS. IT'S A GOOD THING I'M WELL INSURED—HE TOOK MY MOST EXPENSIVE JEWELRY. I HEARD HIM RUN OUT THE BACK DOOR.

6

HE MUST HAVE LEFT SOME FOOTPRINTS IN THE SNOW.

NO, HE DIDN'T— BECAUSE THERE WASN'T ANY ROBBER!

7

**WHY DID TRIXIE SAY THAT?**

# DINING-ROOM THIEF

"It sure is nice of your parents to ask me out to lunch, Honey," Trixie said, looking around the sunny dining room of the Glen Road Inn.

Honey giggled. "Think nothing of it, Trix. It's Cook's day off, and you know how helpless my mother is in the kitchen. She was only too happy when Dad agreed to eat here, instead."

Trixie smiled as Pierre, the head waiter, led them to a table.

They were no sooner seated, however, than Mrs. Boyer, a rich eccentric woman who lived in the inn, hurried to his side. "I lunched at that little window table about half an hour ago," she told him, "and I stupidly left my handbag there. It contained a lot of money. I just looked, but my purse isn't there. Did you find it?"

"No, I didn't, Mrs. Boyer. And no one has turned it in," Pierre said, sounding concerned. "And I'm sure that no one has been near that area since you left it, except Mario, who was your waiter; Bob, the busboy, who clears all the tables; and me."

"No, I didn't clear Mrs. Boyer's table," Bob said, when he and Mario arrived, "so I couldn't have taken anything. I simply didn't have time. Mario had told me to fill some glasses with ice and water to prepare for the lunch rush. After I did that, I had to help in the kitchen. I was gone longer than I expected, and when I came back, the ice in the glasses had melted. The water had overflowed all over the service area, and I had to clean up the mess."

Mario now looked as worried as Mrs. Boyer. "I did tell Bob to fill the water glasses," he said. "I was busy serving my customers. When I realized that he hadn't cleared the window table, I began to do it myself. Pierre came right away to help me. But we didn't see your handbag, Mrs. Boyer, and we didn't take it."

Mrs. Boyer took a deep breath. "In that case," she said sadly, "I'll have to call the police."

Trixie leaned forward. "Excuse me, Mrs. Boyer," she said, "but if you think about it, you'll realize who must have stolen your purse."

Whom did Trixie suspect, and why?

# MISSING PARTNERS

Mart and his friend Bob Hubbell are always having "word" contests. They challenge each other to see who can finish word games like this pairing list first. Try to provide the missing partner for each of these words. Some of them are very easy. Some are not! What's your time score?

1. NUTS and _ _ _ _ _ _
2. BARNUM and _ _ _ _ _ _ _ _
3. STARS and _ _ _ _ _ _ _ _
4. MICKEY and _ _ _ _ _ _ _
5. DONNY and _ _ _ _ _ _
6. BERT and _ _ _ _ _ _
7. ANDROCLES and

   _ _ _  _ _ _ _
8. ROY and _ _ _ _ _
9. PENCIL and _ _ _ _ _ _
10. LAND and _ _ _ _
11. HORSE and _ _ _ _ _ _
12. SHOW and _ _ _ _ _
13. RISE and _ _ _ _ _ _
14. BACON and _ _ _ _ _
15. UPS and _ _ _ _ _ _
16. REST and

    _ _ _ _ _ _ _ _ _
17. KISS and _ _ _ _ _
18. BY and _ _ _ _ _ _

19. UP and _ _ _ _ _ _ _
20. MILK and _ _ _ _ _ _
21. HERE and _ _ _ _ _ _
22. SHIVER and _ _ _ _ _ _
23. ARCHIE and _ _ _ _ _ _
24. STOP and _ _
25. THUNDER and

    _ _ _ _ _ _ _ _ _
26. SOW and _ _ _ _ _
27. READ and _ _ _ _ _ _
28. BALL and _ _ _ _ _ _ _
29. BED and _ _ _ _ _ _
30. RHYTHM and _ _ _ _ _ _
31. HANSEL and _ _ _ _ _ _ _
32. LIFE and _ _ _ _ _ _
33. BRUSH and _ _ _ _ _
34. HORSE and

    _ _ _ _ _ _ _ _
35. SOAP and _ _ _ _ _ _
36. TOOTH and _ _ _ _ _

# DI'S MEMORY SHARPENER

Di cut out pictures of objects, put them on a large sheet of paper, and attached it to the clubhouse door. She asked the other Bob-Whites to study it carefully for one minute. Then she took it down and gave each of them a list of questions to answer.

If you'd like to try her memory sharpener, here it is. Study it for a full minute, then turn the page and see how many of the questions you can answer without looking back.

(HINT: Some objects answer more than one question.)

Remembering that some objects answer more than one question, what did you see that

1. lays eggs?
2. can be read?
3. is useful for walking on snow?
4. gives out music and words?
5. is often made of clay?
6. is useful for riding?
7. can be used for cleaning up crumbs?
8. is useful for watering gardens?
9. can be used in a sport?
10. is often worn around the neck?
11. can be used for its juice?
12. is useful when painting ceilings?
13. has four wheels?
14. hops around?
15. sometimes contains letters?
16. has a bow?
17. can be lighted?
18. will keep your ears warm?
19. tells you the time?
20. honks?

# TRIXIE'S HIDDEN-ANSWER QUIZ

With the help of Trixie's clues, can you discover what is out of place in each group? If you circle the correct letters, they will spell the name of the bird world's "champion weight lifter."

1. Which shelter can disappear in a way none of the others can?

   a. brick mansion    k. wooden stable    c. snow igloo
             b. cloth tent    l. stone garage

2. All perform the same task, but which does it in a different way?

   m. newspaper    o. book    d. billboard    r. radio    e. pamphlet

3. All of these can move, but which one can depart voluntarily?

   f. ketch    s. yawl    e. dinghy    a. dingo    n. dory

4. All are birds, but which can do something none of the others can do?

   a. kiwi    s. penguin    i. ostrich    d. emu    n. condor

5. Which of these is very different from the rest?

   b. nonillion    e. vermillion    n. octillion
      l. quadrillion    k. undecillion

# QUIZ FOR COGITATORS

"A girl told us something in class today that seemed absolutely impossible," said Trixie. "She said it was a fact, though. And our teacher said it was a fact. All we had to do was figure out how it could be so. And we did—but I began to think it would be well into this new year before I caught on to the secret of finding the answer."

This is what Trixie's classmate had said: "Last week I was thirteen years old. Next year I will have my sixteenth birthday."

How can that be so?

# POOR LOSER

Something had happened on the school parking lot. A crowd of students had gathered there, and Trixie and Honey hurried off the school bus and ran to join them.

"What's going on?" Trixie asked Dave Andersen, one of her classmates. "Has there been an accident?"

"It wasn't any accident!" Dave answered angrily. "Bernie Judd just drove his car over my new bike. I was the only witness, but I'm sure he did it on purpose!"

Honey gasped. "But why would Bernie do a mean thing like that?"

"He's mad because I ran against him for class president and won," Dave told them. "He said I'd be sorry if I didn't pull out of the election, and this must be what he meant! Well, he's going to pay me for a new bike!" Dave clenched and unclenched his fists angrily, then stalked away.

Bernie, the school bully, merely sneered. "I'm

not paying for anything," he announced. "All I was doing was looking for an empty parking place. When I spotted this one, I drove forward into it. All at once, I felt something crunch under my wheels. I was already braking, so the car stopped immediately. If His Majesty the class president hadn't been so stupid as to leave his bike where it could get run over, it wouldn't have happened. I'm not buying him a new bike! No, sirree!"

Trixie looked at the ground to see for herself what had happened. The bike, a mass of twisted metal, lay crushed under the back wheels of Bernie's old jalopy.

"It looks as though Bernie's telling the truth for once," Honey exclaimed. "Don't you think so, Trix?"

"No, Honey," Trixie said slowly, "Bernie's just a poor loser. He wrecked Dave's bike on purpose, and he lied about what happened here. I think he's going to have to pay up, after all."

How did Trixie know that Bernie was lying?

# HELP!

"What in the world are you two doing?" Trixie exclaimed.

Honey, facing Jim, was waving her arms overhead from side to side. She laughed. "We're practicing ground-to-air signals in case an emergency comes up."

"And it just might," Trixie said. "We could be marooned on an island, or— Gleeps! I should learn them, too!"

"Here they are," said Jim. "See if you can match the signals with the meanings."

1. Aid Needed Urgently
2. Do Not Try to Land
3. Drop Message
4. Pick Us Up
5. All Well
6. Land Here
7. Yes
8. No

# ANIMALS—STORYBOOK AND OTHERWISE

"How about an animal quiz as a game for the party, Dan?" Jim suggested. "For example, Who is the storybook animal known mostly for his grin?"

"Who is— Oh, I know!" Dan answered. "That's a good idea. And I just thought of two more animals."

"I can think of three," Di put in. "No, four. . . ."

1. Who *is* the storybook animal known mostly for his grin?

2. What storybook animal traveled far, with several companions, seeking courage?

3. What animal, built of wood, led to the downfall of a city?

4. Who is the cartoon animal that became known as an "ambassador of happiness"?

5. Who was the animal raised from cubhood by humans who trained her for jungle life?

6. What nursery-rhyme animal performed a fantastic deed in space that has almost, but not quite, been duplicated by man?

7. What animal heroine of movies and television has had both male and female replacements for many years?

8. What animal hero of a modern story and song is famous for the unusual color of a certain part of his face?

9. Who is the animal recognized almost everywhere for his help in preventing forest fires?

10. What great winged mythical animal is also a constellation?

# THE STOLEN HORSE

**1.** TRIXIE! COME QUICK! SOMEBODY STOLE SUNNY FROM OUR STABLE!

**2.** I WENT TO TAKE HIM TO THE WHEELERS' STABLE WHILE WE'RE GONE, AND HE WASN'T IN HIS STALL. HE WASN'T ANYWHERE! OH, TRIXIE, WHAT'LL I DO? I CAN'T GO ON THE TRIP TOMORROW IF SUNNY'S MISSING!

**3.** THERE ARE TOO MANY HOOFPRINTS AND FOOTPRINTS HERE TO TELL ANYTHING, TRIXIE.

MAYBE SOMEONE IN THE HOUSE SAW SOMETHING.

**4.** I'M SORRY, MISS DIANA, BUT I'VE BEEN ENTIRELY OCCUPIED WITH MATTERS FOR YOUR TRIP TOMORROW. I'VE HAD NO TIME TO PEER OUT THE WINDOWS.

**(5)** THE ONLY THING I NOTICED WAS A VAN FROM THE FURNITURE STORE IN TOWN. IT HAD MOTOR TROUBLE, AND THE DRIVER SURE BANGED AROUND UNDER THE HOOD FOR A LONG TIME.

I HEARD AN ICE-CREAM TRUCK, TOO, BUT I DIDN'T SEE IT.

**(6)** MAYBE YOUR NEW GARDENER SAW SOMETHING.

I DOUBT IT. HE WAS WORKING ON THE OTHER SIDE OF THE HOUSE. BUT WE CAN ASK HIM.

**(7)** NO, I DIDN'T SEE ANYTHING SUSPICIOUS. I DID SEE A BOY THAT LOOKS LIKE YOU, MISS, RIDING THAT WAY ON A BICYCLE.

THAT MUST'VE BEEN MART. MAYBE HE SAW SOMETHING, TRIX. LET'S GO CALL YOUR HOUSE.

**(8)** I JUST THOUGHT OF SOMETHING, DI! I THINK I KNOW HOW SUNNY WAS STOLEN. WE WON'T CALL MART— WE'LL CALL SERGEANT MOLINSON!

**WHOM DID TRIXIE SUSPECT? HOW WAS SUNNY STOLEN?**

47

# THE FIRE

Mrs. Pritchard glared at Bobby Belden, then at his sister, Trixie. It was a blistering day outside, but it was cool in the Pritchard house in spite of the smell of smoke that wafted through.

"I tell you, your little brother set the fire in the lot next door," Mrs. Pritchard said angrily. "I insist that he be punished!"

"I didn't do it!" cried Bobby. His voice shook, and he backed up against Trixie as if he needed support.

Trixie put her hands on Bobby's shoulders and looked at Mrs. Pritchard with great concern. Then she looked around the big living room, at the hulking, dark, old-fashioned furniture, the heaps of dusty books, and the ancient window air conditioner.

"He should be taught a lesson," Mrs. Pritchard snarled. "I heard him run down the alley behind the house, and just a few minutes later, I smelled smoke and saw flames. That grass is tinder dry in this weather. It's a miracle my house didn't catch fire!"

"But I didn't do it!" Bobby cried again. "I didn't come until I heard the sirens. Then I saw the smoke and I came. I was playing in Galt's woods."

"A likely story!" scoffed Mrs. Pritchard, who was widely known in Sleepyside as a person who disliked children. "I heard you *before* the fire started. You went by like a jackrabbit, just itching to get into trouble."

Mrs. Pritchard mopped at her face with a handkerchief. "It's starting to get warm in here," she whined. "I wish the crew from the electric company would hurry and replace the wire that burned out when the big tree caught on fire, so I can turn the air conditioner on again."

"Mrs. Pritchard, did you actually *see* Bobby go by?" Trixie asked.

"N-No," admitted the old woman. "But I heard him. And that was just minutes before the fire started."

"You're mistaken," Trixie said. "I don't think you heard him at all. You couldn't have! And I'll soon show you why!"

How did Trixie show Mrs. Pritchard?

# ABOUT HORSES

"Does anybody around here know anything about horses?" Regan asked as the B.W.G.'s entered the stable.

"Not nearly as much as you do," Brian answered. "Why? What's up?"

"Well, you all seem so interested in quizzes these days, and I found this one about horses—" Regan took a paper from his pocket.

Trixie peered at it, then said, "Try it on us while we groom our horses."

1. What game on horseback was played in Persia 2,500 years ago and is played today in the United States?

2. What is the oldest and purest breed of horses?

3. Is it true that there are no really wild horses left in the world?

4. What animals are related to the horse?

5. How many toes does a horse have on each foot?

6. Which of the following is a four-beat gait (i.e., four hoof-beats can be heard)?
   a. trot    b. gallop    c. pace    d. canter

7. Is the palomino one of the largest breeds of horses?

8. Which breed of horse is recognized for its use of these gaits: running walk, flatfoot walk, and rocking-chair canter?

9. Which breed of horse has long held the world weight-pulling record?

10. Which breed is the world's fastest horse?

# SODA-POP MIX-UP

While Bobby Belden was watching a filmed commercial about one of his favorite kinds of soft drink, the television went haywire.

If you put the frames of the film in the order the actions really happened, the letters in the upper left corners will spell out the name of the flavor of the drink. What is it?

# The Case of the Two Winners

"It says *what?* Are you serious?" Brian Belden stared at his sister, Trixie, and at the letter that quivered in her fingers. "Mart, did you hear what I heard?"

Mart Belden nodded. "I heard, but indubitably my auricular orifices deceived me. Never was there a more unlikely—"

"Stop it, you two." Honey Wheeler threw her arms around her best friend's shoulders. "Ignore them, Trixie. Read the letter out loud so that we can all hear what it says."

Trixie's usually confident voice shook as she began: " 'It is a pleasure to inform you that you have won first place in the Junior Women's Club poster contest. The judges commend you for your exceptional and timely treatment of the theme, Communication. . . .' "

"Oh, Trixie," Honey said, "I'm so proud of you."

"All of us are," said another voice, and Jim Frayne, Honey's adopted brother, strolled into the Belden living room. "I just heard the news from your mom, Trix. It's great!"

Trixie felt a blush starting, much to her annoyance. "They've probably made a mistake," she said. "Tomorrow, I'll get another letter telling me to tear up the first one and—"

"Trixie, don't talk like that!" Honey broke in. "The letter says that you're invited to the Club dinner October twenty-ninth to get a hundred-dollar prize! What are you going to do with it?"

Trixie looked pleased at the question that diverted attention from her artistic capabilities. "Well," she said, "you all know Marcy Jones, don't you?"

"Of course we know her," Mart replied. "Marcy just won the state Miss Black Teen contest. She's made our class famous."

"And she's absolutely beautiful and dances like a dream," Honey added. "What about her?"

"Well," Trixie explained, "she leaves a week from Saturday for the national contest in Los Angeles, and yesterday I heard her say that she was going to borrow her cousin's luggage to take on the trip. Her parents have spent so much on dancing costumes and other things for the contest that she refuses to let them buy new luggage, too. I thought that since her classmates are so proud of her—"

"We'll buy some luggage for her," Jim interrupted. "Terrific!"

"Oh, Trixie, that's a great idea!" Honey exclaimed. "There's a gorgeous red plaid set in the Teen Town department store in White Plains. People can contribute what they want, and we'll request a special assembly in Marcy's honor just before she leaves."

"What a nice idea!" It was Mrs. Belden, carrying a tray of chocolate cake and tall glasses of milk. "Break time, everyone," she said. "Have a snack while I tell Trixie about her party."

"Party!" Trixie gasped. "For me? Oh, no!"

"Oh, yes." Moms smiled. "It's not every day we discover an artist in our family. It will be a very little party," she added gently, for Trixie looked as if she were about to bolt. "Since the public isn't invited to the Club dinner, your father and I want to do something special for you afterward. We'll have the Bob-Whites, of course, and the Wheelers and—"

"Oh, Moms," Trixie groaned.

"It'll be fun," Honey told her. "We want to

celebrate with you, too. This is one of the biggest things that's ever happened to any of us."

"Agreed," Brian said solemnly. "Here's to our resident celebrity!" And they all settled down to enjoy the cake.

The next morning, it seemed as if everyone at school had heard the news. Marcy Jones was waiting inside the front door.

"Oh, Trixie, I'm almost as excited as I was when I won the Teen contest," she cried. "I never knew you were an artist."

"She's surprised us all." Trixie turned to see Nick Roberts smiling at her. "Congratulations."

Nick was a fine artist himself and planned to make art his career. Trixie smiled her thanks. The smile stayed there all morning as classmates and teachers stopped in the halls to offer their congratulations. It didn't fade until art class, when Mr. Crider said how pleased he was that Trixie had won the contest and that another class member, Jay Miller, had taken an honorable mention.

"I'm afraid I didn't realize myself how good Trixie's poster was." Mr. Crider smiled. "Perhaps the simplicity of detail. . . ."

"Do you mean that Trixie is a primitive, Mr. Crider?" It was Jay Miller, his face twisted in an unpleasant grin.

"I mean that qualified judges have recognized

something special in Trixie's work," Mr. Crider said evenly. "And I hope every one of you is as happy for her as I am."

The class applauded, but a cloud had settled over Trixie's day. It darkened after class when she found Jay standing just outside the door.

"Congratulations on your beginner's luck," he said coldly. "Because that's what it is. My poster was good—really good—and we both know that yours wasn't any good at all."

Trixie felt as if she had been slapped. She was still standing there, stunned, when Honey came out of the room across the hall and joined her.

"Trixie, what's the matter? Did someone say something mean?"

Trixie took a deep breath. "Nothing's the matter," she said firmly. "Have you talked to anyone about the surprise for Marcy?"

"It's all settled," Honey told her happily. "Our class has formed a committee to collect contributions. They all think your giving your award to the fund is the nicest thing they've ever heard of."

Trixie shook her head. "There's nothing special about giving the prize to the fund," she said, so seriously that Honey stopped short. "The money isn't important, but—*winning*, Honey— having people think I'm a good artist—that *is* important to me."

Honey put her arm around Trixie's shoulders. "Of course it's important," she said. "Why do you look so sad?"

"I'm not sad," Trixie said. She brushed angrily at her eyes, thinking of Jay. "Let's have lunch, Honey. After all," she added, with a determined change of mood, "even great artists must eat!"

Laughing, they hurried to the cafeteria.

"I'll reserve a table if you'll get soup to go with our sandwiches," Honey offered. "I'll save room for the other Bob-Whites, too."

Trixie found herself in line behind Marcy Jones. "You look as if you're on Cloud Nine these days," she told Marcy. "I'm surprised your feet touch the ground."

Marcy's lovely smile seemed to brighten the whole room. "Every time I think about flying to Los Angeles and competing in front of all those people . . ." she responded gaily. "Oh, Trixie, I *am* excited!"

"Two happy winners!" a sneering voice broke in. "But only one deserved to win. The other has some crazy art judges to thank."

The girls whirled to find Jay Miller in line behind them.

"Don't you dare say that!" Marcy cried. "You haven't any right to criticize. You're a bad loser, that's all!"

"I'll second that." It was Mart, his blue eyes

flashing as he moved up to join the group. "If you haven't anything good to say, I'd suggest you keep quiet, Miller."

Jay threw his tray on the counter and turned away. "Forget it," he snarled. "Who cares about a stupid poster contest, anyway?" He pushed past Mart and stalked out of the cafeteria.

"I care," Trixie said in a soft voice. "If I didn't care, it wouldn't matter what he said."

"Of course you care," Marcy said. "Jay is a mean person, Trixie. Just ignore him."

Now that the unpleasantness was over, Mart resumed his usual role as tease. "You know what they say about absentminded artists, Marcy," he began gravely. "I bet my sister has completely forgotten to deliver the invitation our mother extended this morning. She—and we—would like you to come to our house for a pre-Los Angeles dinner next Wednesday night. Of course," he continued, "that's the night before the awards dinner, so Trixie probably won't be a very good hostess, but the rest of us will make it a real celebration."

"Oh, Marcy, I *did* forget," Trixie moaned. "Can you come?"

"I'd love to," Marcy told them. "I wouldn't miss it for anything."

"Good!" Mart exclaimed. "Join us for lunch, and we'll make plans."

"Is there room for me?" Marcy asked. "You

usually have a pretty crowded table."

"Of course," Trixie replied. "We'd make room anyway, but this week we have space to spare. Di Lynch is in Bermuda with her parents—they took their whole family on a trip to celebrate their wedding anniversary. They even took a tutor along so Di wouldn't fall behind in her work. And Dan Mangan eats early so he can work out in the gym."

During the lunch hour following, the ugly scene with Jay Miller was all but forgotten. The Bob-Whites were in a mood to enjoy the good things that were happening, and they let Trixie and Marcy know how proud they were of them.

Later, as they carried their empty trays to the kitchen pass-through, Marcy said, "I've never felt so good in my life. Sometimes I think, what if I only dreamed that I was going to Los Angeles, and then I woke up. . . . What would I do?"

"You'd just have to find something else good to think about and plan for, I guess," Trixie replied. "But you don't have to worry, Marcy. You've won the state contest, and you're going to Los Angeles—and you're going to win there, too." She squeezed her friend's hand.

"That's right," Honey chimed in. "You and Trixie are never going to forget this October." She hugged them both as she said it, but Trixie felt suddenly uneasy. *I'm telling Marcy not to worry about anything*, she thought, *but I'm worried myself. What's the matter with me?* She suppressed a shiver and hurried after her friends.

It was, indeed, an exciting week. One afternoon after school, Jim drove Trixie and Honey to White Plains to look at the red plaid luggage. Donations for the gift were coming in at a great rate, and with the promise of Trixie's prize money, they felt safe in asking the clerk to put the luggage on layaway.

Another afternoon, a reporter came out to Crabapple Farm to interview Trixie.

"We'll take a picture at the Club dinner," she explained, "but I'd like to get some background for an article."

Trixie answered a number of questions as well as she could, while her little brother, Bobby, stood beside her chair and stared at the reporter with awe.

"Had you painted much before the contest?"

Before Trixie could answer, Bobby piped up. "She draws pictures for me all the time," he said proudly. "The bestest pictures in the whole world. She draws pictures of our dog, Reddy, and the Wheelers' horses, and our house, and—"

"And I think she's very lucky to have a brother like you," the reporter said, chuckling. "May I put your name in my story, too?"

"That's okay," Bobby said generously. The interview ended in laughter.

"It was a good thing he interrupted," Trixie said Wednesday night as the Bob-Whites waited in the Belden living room for Marcy to arrive. "The pictures I'd drawn for Bobby were all I'd ever done before taking Mr. Crider's art class."

"I holped you," Bobby said with satisfaction.

"I guess you did," Brian agreed. "Why don't you 'holp' right now by going out to the road to see if you can find a girl on a red bicycle. Marcy's late," he went on as Bobby raced out the front door.

Trixie looked out a front window. "You know," she said thoughtfully, "I don't remember Marcy ever being late for anything. She takes pride in keeping to her schedule, even though she has dancing and modeling and gymnastics classes to fit in around her school hours."

She watched Bobby turn back toward the house with dragging feet. "Maybe we should drive toward town and look for her."

"It might be a good idea," Jim agreed. His own inclination was to wait a while longer, but he respected Trixie's intuition.

Brian, too, recognized the concern in Trixie's voice. "I'll drive," he said. "We'll probably meet her before we've gone half a mile."

Trixie went to tell her mother where they were

going, and then they all piled into Brian's jalopy. It was nearly dark as they started down Glen Road. The moon was a dim globe behind high clouds, and the wind was rising, bringing with it a first touch of winter, as the headlights probed the dark road.

"Something *is* wrong," Trixie said, when they had ridden a mile. "Marcy was looking forward to tonight as much as we were. She would never be this late if she could help it."

"I'm afraid you're right, Trixie," Honey said nervously.

"Look!" Dan pointed to the left side of the road. "Stop, Brian! There's something there in the ditch!"

The jalopy squealed to a halt, and they all jumped out.

"Oh, no!" Trixie gasped as she got a close look at what Dan had seen. It was a red bicycle, badly crumpled.

"Over here," Brian snapped. He was kneeling in the low ditch, and when the others ran to join him, they saw Marcy lying unconscious, her left leg twisted under her and her right sleeve soaked with blood.

"Get the flashlight and the blanket from the back of the car," Brian ordered. "Quick, Mart!" He folded his own jacket to pillow Marcy's head. "Jim, please go home and call an ambulance.

Here are the keys to my car. You'd better call the police, too."

Trixie, too stunned to move, was grateful for the way Brian took charge. He planned to be a doctor someday, and he could be counted on to do the right thing in a situation like this.

"We can't move her," he said tersely. "That leg looks bad. We'll just have to keep her warm until the ambulance gets here, and I'll see what I can do about her arm. Dan, do you have your pocketknife?"

Quickly, he cut away the jacket sleeve. At the sight of the injured arm, Honey looked away, but Brian gave a sigh of relief. "It's not a bad cut, just a messy one. Does anybody have something I can use to cover it?"

Honey pulled off her scarf and held it out. Brian folded it expertly and carefully wrapped it around Marcy's arm.

For the next twenty minutes, the little group knelt and stood around Marcy. Jim came back with another jacket for Brian and a sterile bandage for Marcy's arm. He'd called Marcy's parents, too. They'd go directly to the hospital.

"It's so awful!" Trixie said. "Her leg . . ." She couldn't bear to think what it would mean if Marcy's leg was broken.

"How c-could she have fallen so hard? Do you think she hit a rock on the road?" Honey asked.

Trixie looked around thoughtfully. Suddenly she hurried back to the red bicycle. It was badly mangled, and at first she doubted that it could yield a clue to what had happened. Then she noticed some white paint on the dented rear fender.

"Honey, Jim, look here!" She pointed at the streak. "That answers your question about what happened. Marcy was thrown off her bike by a hit-and-run car!"

The Bob-Whites stared at each other. Had someone in a white car really hit Marcy and left her there in the dark, alone and injured?

Honey asked anxiously, "Where *is* that ambulance? It seems like hours since we found her."

As if answering her, the thin wail of a siren sounded in the distance.

"Marcy?" It was Mart, still squatting beside the injured girl. "Hey, everybody! She opened her eyes for a second."

Trixie, Honey, and Jim raced back to his side. "It's okay, Marcy," Trixie whispered. "The ambulance will be here in just a minute. . . . Marcy, can you hear me?"

Marcy's lips moved. Trixie put her head close to her friend's. "Marcy, did you see the car that hit you?"

"Trix, not now," Brian protested, then stopped because Marcy's eyes had opened wide.

"Yes." She grimaced. "It stopped and backed

up close to me. But no one got out." Her eyes widened. "My leg— It hurts!"

Lights flashed as the ambulance and a police car drew close. "Marcy—" Trixie began, but Brian interrupted.

"No more questions," he said firmly. "You're tiring Marcy out."

"Trixie?" Marcy's voice was strained through tears. "It was a white car, Trixie. And the license plate had an *E* and a *3* and a *1* on it. It was stopped right in front of my eyes for a minute." She sighed heavily. "It doesn't matter, I guess. Everything's spoiled. . . ."

The ambulance and police car had stopped, and the attendants were hurrying over with a stretcher. "Come on, gang," Dan said. "Let's get into the car and keep out of their way."

Trixie saw a familiar face. "Okay, but first I'm going to tell Sergeant Molinson what Marcy told us," she said.

After taking the rest of the Bob-Whites back to Crabapple Farm, Brian and Trixie drove to the hospital. It was nearly one in the morning when they returned.

"Marcy's going to be okay," Brian said, "but her leg is broken. She'll be in a cast for weeks."

"The contest!" Honey cried. "Marcy won't be able to go to Los Angeles Saturday."

Brian shook his head. "No, she won't," he said.

"But she's alive, and that's what matters most."

All through the rest of that night, as Trixie lay in bed unable to sleep, she kept hearing Brian's words. Marcy had wondered how she could bear it if she woke up to find the contest nothing but a dream. Well, it had happened. There'd be no contest for Marcy. But she was alive, she would recover, and that *was* what mattered most.

Honey's voice was foggy with sleep when she answered Trixie's call early the next morning. "I kept dreaming—" she began, but Trixie cut in.

"Honey, how many people do you know who have white cars?"

There was a short silence. "Trixie, *lots* of people have white cars. There's old Mrs. Gates, and Mr. Tarman, the postmaster, and— Oh, Trix, you mustn't think about the accident today . . . not the day of the awards dinner. Sergeant Molinson will find the driver. Marcy wouldn't want anything to spoil today, even if . . ."

"Even if her own big day has been ruined," Trixie finished. "Honey, *I've* thought of a white car Sergeant Molinson isn't going to find listed when he checks license numbers. Because it's a Wisconsin plate, not New York."

"Wisconsin?" Honey was puzzled. "Who do you know from Wisconsin, Trixie?"

"Jay Miller's brother Tom," Trixie told her excitedly. "That is, I don't know Tom Miller, but I know his car, and so do you. He's living in Wisconsin, but a month ago he drove out here and left his car with his parents while he went to Europe on business. Jay drives it to school once in a while. He doesn't drive it often—I bet his brother didn't give him permission to use it—but he does drive it."

"Oh, Trixie," Honey protested, "you don't think Jay— I mean, he's not a very nice person, but I don't believe he could be a hit-and-run driver."

"*You* never think *any* person could be that mean," Trixie said sharply, "but someone was, Honey. And I'm going to get Brian to take me to school early this morning to check the student parking lot. If Tom Miller's license has an *E* and a *3* and a *1* on it, I'll call Sergeant Molinson right away. Do you want to go with us?"

"Of course I do," Honey said. "But, oh, Trixie, I wish you didn't have anything on your mind except the art award."

Three quarters of an hour later, Brian turned into the school parking lot. "No white cars in sight," he commented.

"The Millers' blue sedan isn't here, either," Trixie said. "That's what Jay usually drives."

Several more cars turned into the lot before Trixie let out her breath in a long, disappointed sigh. "Here he comes," she said. "In the sedan."

"Of course," Brian said slowly, "if the white car is scratched, Jay might be afraid to drive it today. He'd probably pound out the dent and touch it up, so no one would ask questions."

"That's right!" Trixie exclaimed. "We have to get a look at that car before he—"

Brian raised a warning hand. "Trixie, don't get involved. You've got enough to think about today."

Trixie nodded. "It *is* a special day," she agreed. "But this was supposed to be a special time for Marcy, too. And we're her friends, so—"

"So we'll talk about it tomorrow," Brian finished. "If the police haven't found the white car by then, we can suggest that they take a look at Jay's brother's car. Okay?"

Honey nodded quickly, but Trixie didn't answer. And all morning long, she went through her classes in a kind of trance. Her mind went from Marcy to the white car and then to the Club dinner. When she thought of the poster contest, the butterflies in her stomach became almost unbearable.

Lunch was a subdued hour, with the conversation centering mostly on ways the Bob-Whites might help to cheer Marcy. When the boys left, Trixie turned to Honey.

"I don't have a class next hour, Honey, and neither do you. If I sit in study hall just thinking about Marcy and the white car and not doing anything, I'll absolutely explode."

"But what can you do?" Honey demanded.

"I can go out to the Millers' estate and look for the car," Trixie said promptly. "I'm going to get permission at the office to leave the building for an hour, and then I'm going to borrow a bike from someone. Do you want to come along?"

"Oh, Trixie, the police will go—"

Trixie shook her head. "Jay may have the car fixed so there isn't any proof of an accident. For all we know, he's working on it this very minute. I don't see him in the cafeteria, do you?"

Twenty minutes later, the two girls were approaching the Miller estate on borrowed bicycles. Jay's house was huge, its red brick warm in the autumn sun. A low stone wall enclosed the property on three sides, and the fourth side was bordered by thick woods.

"We'll leave the bikes hidden in the brush," Trixie said.

"I don't like this," Honey said nervously. "We don't have any right to be here."

Trixie led the way through the woods. "We're not going to do any harm, Honey," she insisted. "And if we're wrong about what we suspect, no one else will ever know how we misjudged Jay."

The stretch of lawn between the woods and the four-car garage looked endless. "I think I'd better do this alone, Honey," Trixie said. "I thought we could both get up to the garage window, but that would be too dangerous. I'll just run right across the lawn and hope no one in the house happens to be looking out."

Before Honey could protest, Trixie was skimming across the grass. When she reached the garage, she sank down and worked her way to the first window. Cautiously she raised her head and peered in. There was nothing to be seen but the blue station wagon, its bulk blocking her view of whatever else the garage contained.

*I'll have to get inside if I'm going to find out anything*, Trixie thought as she moved along the wall to a corner and peered around it. The doors of the garage stood open. The first space beside the station wagon was empty, and so was the farthest section of the garage. Between the two empty places stood Tom Miller's white sports car.

Trixie took a deep breath and stepped out to look at the car's license plate: *E37-142.*

*I knew it! Now if I can just get a look at the right fender . . .* Trixie was halfway to the car, when a figure suddenly stood up on the other side. It was Jay Miller, a can of spray paint in his hand and a look of pure rage in his eyes.

"What are you doing here?" he roared. He came toward her threateningly.

*I can't leave now*, Trixie thought, *not until I*

*know* . . . She ran forward and around Jay. His arm swung up, and a white mist exploded from the paint can.

"I'll get you, you little snoop!" he bellowed.

Trixie turned then and dashed across the lawn toward the woods. Jay lunged after her, but when he saw Honey suddenly erupt from her hiding place in the brush, he stopped. The two girls plunged into the woods.

"Are you all right, Trixie?" Honey cried. "I couldn't move—I was so terrified when I heard Jay's voice."

"I'm all right," Trixie panted. They reached their bicycles and pedaled away from the Miller estate as fast as they could go.

When they reached the busy main road, Trixie stopped worrying about whether Jay was following them.

"Slow down, Honey," she begged. "I have to catch my breath."

They stopped for a moment at the side of the road. "Jay sounded furious!" Honey exclaimed. "And, Trixie, what's that white stuff all over your jacket?"

Trixie looked down. "I guess it's evidence. Jay was using spray paint on the car, Honey. And just before he sprayed the paint at me, I saw what he was working on—a couple of long red scratches on the fender!"

It was exactly seven-thirty when Trixie walked up the steps of the Junior Women's Club building. The telephone call to Sergeant Molinson was behind her. As usual, the sergeant had scolded her for getting involved in an investigation instead of calling him, but he'd also promised to go out to the Miller estate immediately.

Her family's fond teasing and the excitement of getting dressed for the evening were behind her, too. Right now, she knew, her mother and Honey were busy getting ready for the party in her honor. Jim had driven her into town and would be back later to take her home. But for now she was alone, and the thought of what was about to happen filled her with a deep excitement she could share with no one.

The big, brightly lit dining room was filled with women. At the far end, on a dais, was the speaker's podium, and behind it was a semicircle of posters on easels.

"Welcome." A red-haired young woman shook Trixie's hand. "You must be Trixie Belden. I'm Grace Newcomb, the contest chairman. Your poster is marvelous!" She drew Trixie into the room. "The idea of using a communications satellite as your central symbol caught the judges' attention immediately. How did you ever think of it?"

Trixie was too excited to remember. "Well—"

she began, but at that moment the newspaper photographer came up.

"I'd like a shot of Miss Belden with her prize-winning poster," she said.

"Fine." Mrs. Newcomb pointed to the dais. "The poster is on display with the other winners up there."

Trixie looked. "N-No, it isn't," she said.

Mrs. Newcomb put an arm around her. "Yes, it is, dear. Right in the center—with the blue ribbon on it."

Trixie felt as if she might faint. "Th-That's not my poster," she said shakily. "It's a communications satellite, but it's not mine." She took a deep breath. "Mrs. Newcomb, I couldn't paint anything that beautiful if I tried for a hundred years!"

The next few minutes were a nightmare. Trixie stood, stricken, unable to look at the sympathetic faces turned toward her as the news began to travel around the room. Mrs. Newcomb frantically searched for the list of entries.

"You see, we grouped the posters by subject," she told Trixie. "Telephone, television, books, and so forth. Only you and Nick Roberts used a communications satellite as the subject. I just can't believe that we—"

Trixie's eyes filled with tears. "Nick Roberts is the best artist in Sleepyside Junior-Senior High

School," she said. "The labels must have gotten switched when you were sorting them."

"Oh, my dear!" Mrs. Newcomb took Trixie's arm and led her into a little side room. "I'm so sorry. I'll call Nick right now and get this straightened out."

Trixie watched Mrs. Newcomb's face as the woman listened to Nick Roberts describe his poster. Clearly, the prizewinner was his. *Not that it matters whose it is,* Trixie thought. *It's not mine. They never considered giving me a prize. Not even an honorable mention.* And then she was crying openly at the thought of her family and friends waiting at home to congratulate her.

Mrs. Newcomb explained to Nick what had happened and asked him if he could come to the Club building right away. "We're going to give Trixie special recognition, too, of course," she said. "We feel just terrible—"

It was the final humiliation. A "special recognition" to soothe her feelings! Trixie jumped up and ran out of the little office. A moment later, she was running down the street, sobbing bitterly in the cool October night.

It had been the most wonderful thing that had ever happened to her, and now it was the worst. *Everybody will be sorry for me and wonder how I could be so dumb as to believe I was an artist,* she thought.

A tall building loomed in the dark ahead, and Trixie recognized the hospital. Inside it, she thought, there was one person who would know exactly how painful this disappointment was. Dabbing at her eyes, she turned into the lobby and got Marcy's room number at the front desk.

Upstairs, her friend lay so still that at first Trixie thought she was asleep. One leg, encased in plaster, was suspended at an angle, and her arm was heavily bandaged.

"Marcy? Hi. I just—I just wanted to tell you how sorry I am about—everything."

"Hi, Trixie." Marcy's voice was strained, its bubbling vitality drained away. "I thought you'd be getting your award now. *One* of us is having a good week, anyway."

"No," Trixie replied. "We're both having a bad one." She hesitated, telling herself that it had been a mistake to come, that Marcy didn't need any more bad news. But she couldn't stop now.

"I know I shouldn't bother you with my problems, Marcy," she said, "but you're the only one who can understand how I feel. Do you mind?"

Marcy shook her head. "What is it, Trixie? Tell me."

When the story was finished, the girls stared at each other in silence. "I'm really sorry, Trixie," Marcy murmured at last.

"It's a lot worse for you; I know that," Trixie

said. "Missing the contest and being hurt and everything. I don't know how you can stand it."

"I cried all morning," Marcy admitted. "I still feel like crying. My mother says people mature through misfortune, but I don't see—" She stopped, and her eyes widened. "I just thought of something. All my life, people have been praising my looks and my dancing, but tonight is the very first time anyone came to me with a problem because she thought I'd understand. It's a good feeling, Trixie. I like it! Maybe we'll both be better people because we've had some bad times."

"Marcy, you're wonderful! You really are," Trixie said thoughtfully. She pointed into the mirror over the dresser at the end of the bed. "Look. Did you ever see such a gruesome pair?"

Two drooping, tear-stained faces were reflected there, the expressions identical. After a moment, two tremulous smiles appeared.

"If there were a contest for Miss Teen-Age Misery, I think we'd tie for first prize," Marcy said, with the smallest quiver in her voice. "And I don't want the title!" She reached for Trixie's hand. "Remember the day I said I was afraid I might wake up and find that winning the Teen contest was a dream? You said that if that happened, I'd just have to find something else good to think about. You were right, Trix. I'm going to enter the contest again next year for sure, and you have to find something else to plan for, too. You'll be a winner—just wait."

"The World Champion Something-or-Other," Trixie said ruefully. But she was grinning now. "We're having quite an October, aren't we? Honey was right—this is one month we'll never forget!"

A half hour later, the Bob-Whites pulled up in front of the hospital, and Trixie ran out to join them. She had called to tell them that she had stopped in to visit Marcy—nothing more—and had asked them to pick her up at the hospital.

As she approached the car, Mart jumped out and bowed. "Hail to the winner!" he exclaimed. "Your peers salute you!"

"We're proud of you, Trix," Jim said as she climbed into the jalopy.

"Oh, we are!" Honey exclaimed. "And so is Sergeant Molinson. He called to say Jay Miller admitted hitting Marcy. He stopped and was going to help her, but then he panicked and drove away. His father had told him that he wasn't allowed to use his brother's car because he drove too recklessly." She paused, then hurried on. "So now Marcy can concentrate on getting better—I think we should use the luggage money to buy her a new bike, don't you?—and you can concentrate on being a famous artist. Come on, Trixie, tell us every single thing that happened at the

Junior Women's Club tonight."

Trixie took a deep breath. "Well," she said, "it was like this." And she told them, watching their shocked expressions as the story unfolded. Dismay, deep concern, and sympathy were there, too, followed by pride and admiration.

"So I'm not an artist after all," she finished. "There's no use feeling too bad about it. Nick Roberts will have some money for his art school fund, and I—" She felt Honey's hand on hers and Jim's arm around her shoulders. "I'm a winner, too, as long as I have friends and a family who love me the way I am."

There was a long silence, broken by Mart. "If such a happy solution is applicable to you, dearest Beatrix, it applies equally to all of us and is best celebrated by hastening to our humble abode to enjoy the delectable repast proffered by our inestimable parents."

"I'm not sure what you said, Mart," Trixie replied saucily, "but, whatever it was, let's go eat. I'm starved!"

# REGAN'S HELPER?

After Regan's living room walls had been painted, six-year-old Bobby Belden helped his friend restore the room to order. Although he put all but two objects back in their places, he didn't always do it correctly. Can you find all the items in this picture that Bobby has put back but not in just the right way? Which objects didn't get put back at all?

(HINT: One of the items is really a group!)

# FAMOUS PLACES IN THE UNITED STATES

In their travels in the United States, the Bob-Whites have visited three of the famous places included in the quiz below. As you name the places, put a star by the ones *you* have seen.

1. The Gateway Arch, located near the banks of the Mississippi River, is in what city?

2. This island in the San Francisco Bay once had a federal prison located on it.

3. This fort—originally a mission—in San Antonio, Texas, was the scene of a famous battle.

4. The citizens of this city were not allowed to vote for President until 1964.

5. In which eastern city is the United Nations building located?

6. The Golden Gate Bridge connects this western city with Marin County.

7. France gave us this symbol of freedom, a famous landmark that is located in New York harbor.

8. The Pilgrims sailed from Europe on the **Mayflower** and settled here.

9. James Marshall, a carpenter, found gold in the American River at this site.

10. Independence Hall houses the Liberty Bell in this eastern city.

# THE SUSPECT IN THE RESTAURANT

1. THE CONDENSATION OF SOME AQUEOUS VAPOR IS COMMENCING WITH RAPIDITY.

2. IT SURE IS POURING NOW.

I HOPE IT LETS UP SOON. I TOLD MOMS THAT I'D TAKE BOBBY TO VISIT OLD BROM THIS AFTERNOON, AND—

HELP! THIEF!

3. A MAN SNATCHED MY PURSE! HE WENT THAT WAY!

4. YOU CAN CATCH YOUR BREATH WHILE WE CALL THE POLICE FROM HERE.

5. THIS IS SILLY. WE DON'T KNOW WHAT THE MAN LOOKS LIKE.

YEAH—AND EVERYBODY'S RUNNING TO GET OUT OF THE RAIN.

**6** HEY, TRIXIE— THIS WOULD BE A GOOD PLACE FOR A THIEF TO TRY TO HIDE. LET'S GO IN.

**7** YOU CHECK THE MEN'S ROOM, AND I'LL ASK SOME PEOPLE OUT HERE.

**8** NO, I DIDN'T NOTICE ANYONE COME IN RECENTLY, BUT I'VE BEEN BUSY, AS YOU CAN SEE.

**9** SORRY, BUT BETWEEN OUR KIDS AND ALL THE PEOPLE CROWDING AROUND THE DOOR, WE WOULDN'T KNOW IF ANYONE CAME IN LATELY.

**10** I HAVEN'T SEEN ANYONE, AND I'VE BEEN HERE OVER AN HOUR. TRY SOMEPLACE ELSE, KID.

**11** IF THAT GUY IN THE BACK BOOTH TRIES TO LEAVE, DAN, STALL HIM TILL I CAN GET THE POLICE. I'M PRETTY SURE HE'S THE THIEF.

**WHAT MADE TRIXIE SUSPICIOUS OF HIM?**

83

# THE
# MONEY JAR

Trixie Belden ran across the parking lot of Simpson's hardware store just as Mr. Simpson was opening up.

"Hi, Mr. Simpson," she said. "That was some storm last night, wasn't it? Our lights were out from nine until after midnight."

"Lights were out all over town until after midnight," said Mr. Simpson, as Trixie followed him into the store. "What can I do for you, Trixie?" he asked, his voice subdued.

"I want some paint for my bike," Trixie said. "Is there something wrong, Mr. Simpson? You look upset."

"I'm just worried about my nephew, Stevie," Mr. Simpson said. "He slammed out of the house in the middle of that storm last night and was gone for hours. He's really a good kid, but he's got an awful temper. The paint's over there, Trixie. I'll be right with you." Mr. Simpson vanished into the back room.

Trixie had just put a can of blue paint on the counter, when the door opened and Gary Slade came in. He was Mr. Simpson's clerk, and he wasn't a favorite with the young people in the town. He was prissy and overly particular, and he became very nervous if they moved things even a fraction of an inch out of place. He scowled when he saw Trixie. Then he looked up at the big electric clock on the wall. "Eight-oh-two," he said. "I'm late."

Mr. Simpson came out of the back room. His face was ashen. "I can't believe it!" he said in a stunned way.

"What's wrong, Mr. Simpson?" Trixie asked. "What can't you believe?"

"The money jar—that's where I keep the cash that's left in the register at the end of the day! I hid it in the back room last night, as usual, and now it's gone! Steve—" He stopped suddenly.

"Steve!" cried Gary Slade. "That no-good kid! He has a key. He must have sneaked in last night and. . . ."

"No!" Trixie cried. "You have a key, too, Gary Slade, and I know you were here last night after midnight!"

How did Trixie know this?

# DOODLERS' NOODLERS

"Let's make some more sketches for each other to translate into sports terms," Honey suggested. "The ones Jim and Trixie did yesterday were fun, and I've got a basketball term to start us off." She drew a stick figure of a man on a train seat with a ball on the seat beside him.

Di looked at it for a moment. Then she said, "That's a good one—it's 'traveling with the ball.' It makes me think of another basketball term." And she made a quick drawing of her own.

Soon they were all busy making drawings that illustrate sports terms. How many of them can you figure out?

(NOTE: Some terms may apply to more than one sport.)

1. _____ (basketball)   2. _____ (skiing)

3. _____ (bowling)   4. _____ (golf)

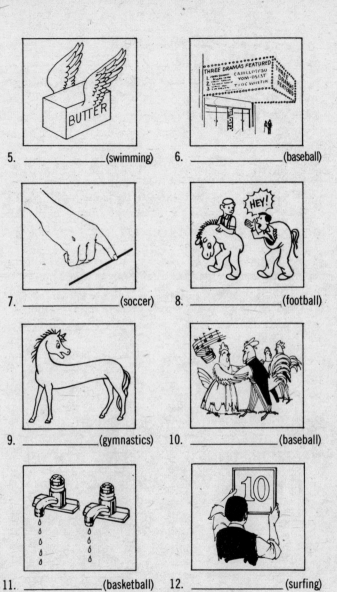

5. _____ (swimming)

6. _____ (baseball)

7. _____ (soccer)

8. _____ (football)

9. _____ (gymnastics)

10. _____ (baseball)

11. _____ (basketball)

12. _____ (surfing)

87

# CRYPTO-TRIXIE

While reading "Miss Lovely's Advice to the Lovelorn" column in the paper, Trixie came upon the following letter. Was she right in suspecting that the letter was more than a matter of the printer's falling asleep? What was Trixie's next step?

Dear Joey,

BLF RWRLG! GSVUYR SZH XZFTSG LM GSZG

R'N FHRMT NB MVDHKZKVI LUURXV ZH Z

UILMG ULI ROOVTZO ARGSVI-HNFTTORMT.

GSZMPH GL BLF, R ZN MLD LM GSVRI GVM-

NLHG-DZMGVW ORHG—ZH Z NZM! RG'H

TLRMT GL YV SZIW ULI NV GL PVVK WRH-

TFRHRMT NBHVOU ZH NRHH OLEVOB NFXS

OLMTVI. JFRXP!—ZIIZMTV ULI C IZBH ZMW

KOZHGRX HFITVIB ZG HG. NZIB'H RNNVWR-

ZGVOB. R DMG GL YV NZWV SZMWHLNV

VMLFTS GL YVXLNV SVZW DZRGVI ZG OZ

TLFINVG IVHGZFIZMG. IRTSG MLD R'N GLL

FTOB GL VEVM DZHS GSVRI WRHSVH!

Love, Miss Lovely

# THE CASE OF
## THE SEMICIRCULAR SUSPECTS

A valuable diamond has been stolen, and Sergeant Molinson has brought five suspects to the police station: Sleazy Sam, Steve the Stoolie, Freddy the Fink, Snipe Thompson, and Pigeon Pete. The suspects are sitting in a semicircle facing the sergeant's desk. Pigeon Pete is just to the left of Sleazy Sam, and Freddy the Fink is just to the right of Snipe Thompson. Steve the Stoolie is sitting next to a wall, with Sleazy Sam closest to him. The guilty suspect is sitting just to the left of the suspect in the center. Who stole the diamond?

## THE CASE OF THE PHANTOM SHOPLIFTER

The Phantom Shoplifter has struck again, this time at a Sleepyside drugstore. Trixie Belden is now on the case, and she has five suspects: Pilfering Paula, Cecily the Snatcher, Devious Dolores, Artful Arlene, and Shifty Sheila. Trixie also has these clues:

1. Both Paula and Arlene are taller than Cecily, but not as tall as Sheila.

2. Three of the suspects, including the two tallest ones, wear earrings.

3. Arlene and Cecily are shorter than Paula, but not as short as Dolores.

4. The two shortest suspects and one of the other suspects wear steel-rimmed glasses.

5. The Phantom Shoplifter wears neither glasses nor earrings.

Who is the Phantom Shoplifter?

# THE
# HOLDUP

Trixie Belden and Diana Lynch turned their bicycles from Main Street onto Elm, then slowed and stopped. A small crowd was gathered in front of the corner church.

"Something's up!" Di said.

"A wedding?" wondered Trixie. Then she saw that it was no wedding. There was a police car at the curb right behind a shabby pickup truck. A man in a paint-spattered coverall stood on the walk talking to two policemen.

"What happened?" Trixie asked a woman at the edge of the crowd.

"A robbery at the supermarket!" whispered the woman. "A man with a gun and a stocking mask forced the manager to open the safe. He got away with a whole sackful of cash. One of the customers saw him run down Elm and dodge into the church."

"Listen," Di said.

The man in the paint-stained coverall looked

smug. "Yeah," he said. "I was working in the church, and I saw a guy with a paper sack come in. He walked right on through and out the back door. I'd say he was average size, and he had brown hair, and . . . and I think he limped a little bit."

The painter turned away and went to his truck. He opened the door on the driver's side, put one polished black oxford under the dashboard, and started to get in.

"Just a minute," a policeman said. "We'll need your name and address, and we'll need you to come down to headquarters to go through some mug books."

"Oh, sure," said the painter easily, getting back out of his truck. "I'll be glad to help in any way I can."

"Maybe he'll find his own picture in the mug books," Trixie said suddenly.

The painter glared. "What do you mean?" he demanded.

"I mean you're no painter!" Trixie declared. "And I'll bet that coverall is padded with the money from the robbery!"

How did Trixie guess that the painter was the holdup man?

# THE EXCHANGE STUDENT

**1** HONEY, WE HAVE TO HELP KIM TSU. THE FAMILY HE LIVES WITH SAY HE STOLE A WALLET.

**2** POOR KIM! IT MUST BE HARD ENOUGH TO LIVE IN A FOREIGN COUNTRY, NOT KNOWING ANYONE, WITHOUT BEING ACCUSED OF STEALING FROM THE FAMILY YOU LIVE WITH...!

**3** WE WERE GETTING DRESSED TO GO OUT WHEN OUR NEIGHBORS CALLED US OVER TO SEE THEIR NEW BABY. WHEN WE CAME BACK, MY WALLET WAS GONE. FROM THE DRESSER.

WE DON'T WANT TO ACCUSE KIM, BUT HE WAS THE ONLY ONE IN THE HOUSE, AND WE COULD SEE THAT NO ONE CAME TO THE DOOR....

**4** PLEASE BELIEVE ME! I DIDN'T TAKE IT! I WAS UPSTAIRS STUDYING WITH THE RADIO ON LOUD TO CROWD OUT THOUGHTS OF HOME.

I BELIEVE YOU, KIM. IN FACT, I'M SURE YOU DIDN'T TAKE IT!

**5** IF THE POLICE HURRY, MAYBE THEY CAN STILL CATCH THE THIEF. KIM WOULDN'T HAVE GONE OUTSIDE, AND COME IN THE WINDOW TO STEAL THE WALLET, SO SOMEBODY ELSE MUST HAVE DONE IT.

**6** DO YOU THINK SOMEONE BROKE IN? THE WINDOW WAS CLOSED. IT STILL IS— OH! IT'S UNLOCKED! THE SCREEN IS LOOSE, TOO!

PLEASE DON'T TOUCH ANYTHING MORE! THERE MAY BE FINGER-PRINTS AND— HELLO! SERGEANT MOLINSON....

**7** WE GOT SOME GOOD PRINTS ON BOTH THE SCREEN AND THE WINDOW IN THE BEDROOM, TRIXIE. GOOD WORK!

**8** I FOUND HER TRYING TO THROW THIS IN A GARBAGE CAN. WILL YOU SEE THAT EVERYTHING IS THERE, SIR?

**9** I'M AWFULLY GLAD THE REAL THIEF WAS CAUGHT. I'M SURE KIM IS, TOO! BUT, TRIXIE, HOW DID YOU KNOW SOMEONE BROKE IN? YOU DIDN'T EVEN GO NEAR THE WINDOW.

## HOW DID TRIXIE KNOW?

# LEGENDS AND FOLKLORE

"You have all been so interested in legends and folklore," the librarian said to the B.W.G.'s one day, "that I decided you'd enjoy this multiple-choice quiz. It gives the first part of a story or legend. Then you choose what you think is the likely ending for each."

## 1. TEOLA AND THE WHITE DEER

Long ago, Teola, daughter of the chief of the Umpqua Indians in Oregon, lay dying of a dreadful illness that threatened to wipe out the entire tribe. Beyond her tepee, men sat around a fire, mourning. Inside, sorrowful women chanted the death song.

Then something happened that filled everyone with wonder. A snow white deer appeared at the edge of the forest, then walked unafraid toward Teola's tepee. Paying no attention to the silently watching men, the deer circled the tepee three times, stopping twice to look in at the dying girl. After circling Teola's tepee the third time, the beautiful animal entered the small dwelling.

Immediately,

a. the deer kissed Teola, then disappeared into the darkness beyond the fire. Teola slowly rose from her sickbed, completely healed.

b. the deer kissed Teola. As soon as it kissed her, she fell into a natural sleep, completely healed, and the deer turned into a handsome brave from a rival tribe. When he and Teola were married, the two tribes lived together in peace.

c. Teola got up from her sick bed and followed the deer into the forest. She was never seen again.

d. the deer kicked Teola in the head, and she died.

94

# 2. OLD STORMALONG
## AND THE OCTOPUS

Once when Old Stormalong, who was no ordinary sailor, was boatswain of a whaler in the middle of the North Atlantic, an octopus took a fancy to clutch onto the anchor of the whaler with half his tentacles. With the other four tentacles, he grabbed hold of the seaweed on a mile of the ocean floor. That gives you some idea of just how huge that octopus was.

But when it came to size, Old Stormalong was no slouch, either. Where ordinary folk used a knife for eating beans, Stormie ate his off an eighteen-foot oar.

Well, Stormalong had no notion of letting that octopus get away with any foolish ideas, so he dove into the murky depths, prepared to have it out with the monstrous sea creature.

The octopus was happy to accept the challenge. There was a terrible struggle, until finally

a. the waiting sailors gave up and left in lifeboats. They knew that Stormie must have met his match—but, it is said, the whaler is still there and the struggle goes on to this day.

b. the octopus won the battle and is often seen in mid-ocean, riding astride Stormalong, dragging the anchor —and the whaler—through the water.

c. Stormie struck a death-dealing blow. The instant the octopus died, a beautiful mermaid appeared and thanked Old Stormalong for releasing her from her prison in the seaweed below.

d. Stormalong climbed into the ship, pulled up the anchor with his bare hands, and told the captain that they could set sail. The octopus? It was a long time before it undid the knots Stormie had tied in its legs.

# THE SHOPPER

Mrs. Wheeler parked in front of the Village Tog Shop. "Thanks for coming to help me pick out Honey's birthday present, Trixie," she said. "Why don't you start looking at the blazers while I make a quick stop at the bank?"

"Okay," Trixie agreed with a smile.

There was a clipping from the *Sleepyside Sun* taped to the shop window. It told how the shop had supplied the clothes for a fashion show given at the Glen Road Inn to benefit the Sleepyside Animal Shelter. A blond woman was reading the story, and she looked around and smiled when Trixie paused to glance at it.

"It must have been a nice affair," the woman said.

"I guess so," said Trixie as she and the woman both entered the shop.

Trixie was trying on a blazer when Mrs. Wheeler came in. As she came toward Trixie, the blond woman stepped into her path.

"Excuse me," the woman said. She held up a long-sleeved blouse with a mandarin collar. "Can you tell me how much this is? I left my glasses at home."

Mrs. Wheeler looked at the price tag. "It's thirty-five dollars," she said.

"So much?" The woman sighed and hung the blouse back on the rack, then started for the door.

Trixie darted forward. "Wait!" she cried. "You dropped something!"

Suddenly Trixie stumbled. She fell forward, her hands clutching at the air. A second later, she was on the floor of the shop. She had seized the woman's handbag as she fell, and it lay open beside her, its contents spilling out.

"I'm so sorry," Trixie said. She scrambled to her knees and began to gather up the woman's things. Then she held up a wallet. "Look! This is just like yours, Mrs. Wheeler!" she cried. "And—and there are three more wallets here. And this necklace still has the price tag on it!"

"You rotten brat!" screamed the woman. "You did that on purpose!" Then she ran out the door.

Trixie *did* stumble on purpose. Why?

# WORD LADDERS

When Brian has all his assignments done before his study-hall period is over, he likes to work on Word Ladders because they help him to look at all sides of a problem—a very good thing for this future doctor to be able to do. He made up this batch of Word Ladders. See if you can use fewer rungs than Brian did in his solutions.

Start with the word at the top (or the bottom) and change just one letter at a time for each rung of the ladder until you reach the other end. Each rung must have a real word on it. If you need more rungs than are shown, that's okay, but when you've done a few, you probably won't need any extras.

> **Sample:**
>
> T E A
> P E A
> P E T
> P O T

| CODE | WILD | FOOT | SONG | SLOW |
|------|------|------|------|------|
| CORE | ---- | ---- | ---- | ---- |
| CORD | ---- | ---- | ---- | ---- |
| WORD | ---- | ---- | ---- | ---- |
|      | TAME | BALL | ---- | ---- |
|      |      |      | BIRD | ---- |
|      |      |      |      | FAST |

# THE MYSTERIOUS MAP

Trixie was ecstatic when she received the following card in the mail. She was sure it was a treasure map—possibly one showing the way to some of Captain Kidd's buried treasure. After she studied it for a few more minutes, she realized that she was completely wrong. She was still excited, though, as she hurried off. Why?

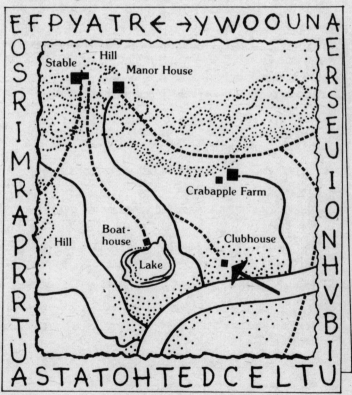

# FOR SUPERSTITIOUS FOLK ONLY

Honey, reading about superstitions, laughed suddenly. "Listen to this, Trixie: 'If you want to become attractive, stand on your head in a corner while eating a chicken gizzard.'"

Trixie regarded Honey solemnly. "Do you think it would work?"

"Oh, Trixie," Honey chided her friend, "you're very attractive just as you are. And I know that Jim thinks so, too. Besides, you aren't really superstitious, are you?"

"No-o-o," Trixie said slowly, "but sometimes I wonder...."

Are *you* superstitious? If so, this quiz is for you. If not, beware! You may pick up a superstition or two!

1. If your palm itches, why should you hurry to put it in your pocket before it touches anything?

2. What can you expect to receive for each white spot on your fingernail?

3. Why are you sometimes happy, and sometimes not, if you sneeze while thinking?

4. What should you do with a four-leaf clover to make sure it does its part to bring you good luck?

5. If you wish on a banana, how do you find out if your wish will come true?

6. Why is it a good idea to have a wish ready to use at once when you wish on a falling star?

7. Why are people with cowlicks sometimes envied?

8. Why are some people glad to get wet in a May rain?

9. What can you do if you want to hasten the departure of bad luck—or make sure it doesn't arrive in the first place?

10. For a little extra good luck . . .

If you answer all thirteen questions correctly, you'll have more good luck than bad for the next thirteen hours.

| What kind of luck may you have if you | GOOD | BAD |
|---|---|---|
| a. see a squirrel crossing your path? | ___ | ___ |
| b. find a pin pointing toward you? | ___ | ___ |
| c. sweep a floor before the sun rises? | ___ | ___ |
| d. rock an empty chair? | ___ | ___ |
| e. watch a person out of sight? | ___ | ___ |
| f. count the cars in a train? | ___ | ___ |
| g. sleep on a table? | ___ | ___ |
| h. hop downstairs on one foot? | ___ | ___ |
| i. take your broom when you move? | ___ | ___ |
| j. see a red bird fly up? | ___ | ___ |
| k. find, pick up, and keep a penny? | ___ | ___ |
| l. catch a falling leaf? | ___ | ___ |
| m. accidentally wear something wrong side out? | ___ | ___ |

## QUICKIE QUIZ #2

Trixie, Jim, Honey, Brian, Mart, Dan, and Di are all members of the Bob-Whites of the Glen, a semisecret club set up to help others and to have fun together. The nephews of Donald Duck and the nieces of Daisy Duck also belong to clubs. Can you give their names and the names of their clubs?

# THE EXTER-MINATORS

Trixie Belden knocked on Mrs. Turner's kitchen door. Then, because it was ajar, she pushed it the rest of the way open and stepped inside.

"Don't stand there, Trixie!" Mrs. Turner cried. "They might come up and get you!"

Trixie blinked. Mrs. Turner was crouched on the kitchen table.

There was a shout from below, and Trixie saw that the door to the basement was open.

"Watch out, Lou!" yelled a man. "He's headed your way!"

Trixie heard a nasty buzzing sound.

"Got him!" shouted a second man.

"Careful!" said the first man. "Watch your hands! There's the sack. Easy now!"

"What's going on?" Trixie asked.

"Snakes!" said Mrs. Turner. "Rattlesnakes in my basement!"

There were footsteps on the cellar stairs. A broad-faced, dark-haired man appeared in the doorway. He had a burlap sack clutched in one grimy fist.

"We got the biggest one, Mrs. Turner," he said cheerfully. He held the sack toward her, and it buzzed loudly. "Want to see him?"

"No!" shrieked Mrs. Turner. "Take it away!"

The man nodded. "Okay. Now don't you worry, Mrs. Turner. By the time we finish, there won't be a snake in the place."

He went back down the stairs, and Trixie heard him and his companions going at their snake hunting with new vigor.

"Mrs. Turner, who is that?" Trixie asked.

"An exterminator." Mrs. Turner shivered. "They're offering free inspections in this neighborhood today. I thought I had a mouse in the basement, so I let them go down to look. They came back up with a snake! Ugh! There's a whole nest of them down there!" Mrs. Turner began to cry.

"How much are they charging?" Trixie asked.

"A hundred dollars," Mrs. Turner said. "They usually charge more for rattlesnakes, but a hundred is all I have in the house."

Trixie started toward the living room. "I'm going to call the police," she said. "Those guys are phonies!"

Why did Trixie distrust the exterminators?

## STOP, THIEF!

STOP, THIEF! SOMEBODY CATCH THAT GUY!

CALL THE POLICE! WE'LL FOLLOW HIM!

HE'S TOO FAST FOR US. WE'LL NEVER CATCH HIM NOW!

MAYBE WE WILL, HONEY. HE JUST TURNED INTO THE MARKET. HE WOULDN'T DARE RUN THROUGH IT WITH HIS MASK ON AND A TELEVISION IN HIS ARMS.

4

He must be in one of the shops—but which one?

I hear a siren, Trixie. Oh, here are the police, now!

5

Joe, you get started checking the shops, while I radio for more help. He's dangerous if he has a gun. You two young ladies go home. We'll take care of it now.

6

I just came out of my meat locker and saw a man in a ski mask in my store. He must be going to rob me! Help me!

7

There's no masked man in that store! **HE'S** the thief! We'd better rescue the owner, quick!

**WHY DID TRIXIE SUSPECT THE MAN FROM THE MEAT STORE?**

# EXPLORING CAVES

"How big can caves get?" Bobby asked as he and his sister and brothers explored a small cave near their home.

"Can you imagine ten football fields put together?" Brian answered. "That's how big some of them are. And they have fantastic things to see in them."

"Sometime, Bobby," Trixie told her little brother, "we'll go and see some of the fabulous caves we've been reading about. Until then. . . ."

Well, until then, how about all of us exploring this quiz about caves?

1. A veiled woman has sat, silent and motionless, in a Pennsylvania cave, waiting—so it is said—for her Indian lover. What is the true explanation for her being there?

2. A cave explorer is called a _____ .

3. One of our Presidents explored a Virginia cave when he was a teen-ager and left his signature with the date. It reads:
   a. George Washington     b. Woodrow Wilson     c. John F. Kennedy
              1748                         1871                        1932

4. The largest cave system in the United States—with an area of more than fifty thousand acres—is in
   a. New Mexico.     b. South Dakota.     c. Kentucky.

5. What important and exciting discovery was made near the Dead Sea in a cave in 1947 by a bedouin goat boy?

6. Is it true that bones of animals living only in the tropics were found in a Maryland cave?

7. Scientific explorers have been unearthing the secrets of caves for several hundred years. True or false?

8. Bats flit about easily in pitch-black caves guided by
   a. the echoes of their sound.      b. their sense of smell.
                    c. their ability to see in the dark.

9. There are some experiences of cave explorers that are similar to those encountered by travelers in outer space. True or false?

10. In addition to the many extraordinary rock formations, there are rivers, waterfalls, and even two lakes in Kentucky's famous Mammoth Cave. True or false?

11. Objects from the world of long ago do not disintegrate in caves as fast as they would if exposed to outside weather. True or false?

12. There are places in which cave explorers must use some of the same equipment that sea divers use: foot fins, aqualungs, rubber diving suits, masks. True or false?

13. Complete the following basic rules of cave exploring:
    Never go into a cave _____ .
    Always carry extra sources of _____ .
    Know the limits of your _____ .

14. What is an easy way to remember the difference between stalactites and stalagmite formations? (Hint: Use the **c** in **stalactites** and the **g** in **stalagmites**.)

15. An Awesome Discovery ————————————

One day, a cowboy in New Mexico saw something in the distance that looked like an erupting volcano. Riding closer, he realized what it was that was "erupting" from a hole in the ground.

The "hole in the ground" turned out to be the still-awesome Carlsbad Caverns—but what did the "volcanic eruption" turn out to be?

# THE
# NEPHEW

"You mean you just found out you have a nephew?" Trixie Belden asked. She stared at Mrs. Forsythe. "That's wonderful!"

The old lady smiled. "It *is* wonderful, isn't it?" she replied. "He's my brother Henry's son, of course. His name is Henry Soames, too, and he called a little while ago from Grand Central Station. He'll be here on the next train. I wonder if he looks like my brother. I hope he does."

"But how did he find you?" Trixie asked. "You always said your brother ran away from home when you were just a little girl. And you grew up in Albany. If your brother never came back, how did his son know you live here in Sleepyside?"

Mrs. Forsythe smiled again. "He saw my picture in that senior-citizen magazine. You remember—they came and photographed me after my quilt won the prize at the county fair."

Mrs. Forsythe took a dog-eared magazine from the coffee table. It was already opened to a page where she smiled out of a full-color photograph. In the picture, the old lady held up her prize quilt. The caption read: "Mrs. Evalina Forsythe shows the quilt that won first prize at the Westchester County Fair. Mrs. Forsythe, a retired schoolteacher, makes her home in Sleepyside-on-the-Hudson in a cottage she shared for more than thirty years with her late husband, James."

There was a knock at the door, and Mrs. Forsythe hurried to answer it. A handsome, ruddy-faced man stood on the threshold. "Aunt Evalina!" he said. Then he grinned. "You look just the way I imagined you would. Dad talked so much about you!"

Trixie tiptoed away, out the back door and home. She found her father sitting in the kitchen. "Mrs. Forsythe's nephew is visiting her," she told him, "and I think he's a phony. I think we should call the police and have them check him out."

Why was Trixie suspicious of Mrs. Forsythe's nephew?

# TRIXIE AND HONEY'S REVENGE

"Okay, Mart," said Trixie. "You're always using big words to tease us, so here's where we get our revenge. Honey and I put some familiar sayings into outsize words. Can you translate them and match them with their originators?"

a. P. T. Barnum      f. Big Bad Wolf

b. Chicken Little      g. Marie Antoinette

c. John F. Kennedy      h. Harry Truman

d. Douglas MacArthur      i. Neil Armstrong

e. Horace Greely      j. Little Jack Horner

1. "The firmament is plummeting."

2. "There's an easily outmaneuvered Homo sapien brought into existence every sixtieth part of an hour."

3. "What an exemplary stripling am I."

4. "Sally forth in an Occidental direction, adolescent fellow; sally forth in an Occidental direction."

5. "Allocate to them the privilege of assimilating a repast of torte."

6. "I'll utilize a current of vapor to exterminate your domicile."

7. "One diminutive advance of a lower extremity for a bipedal primate mammal . . ."

8. "Interrogate not how your **patria** can convey succor to you . . ."

9. "If you can't tolerate the torridity, do not tarry on the premises where comestibles are concocted."

10. "Superannuated combatants never encounter demise."

# EMBEZZLER!

An embezzler was somewhere in the bank lobby. As he scanned the lobby on the closed-circuit television, Sergeant Molinson had very little trouble spotting the criminal employee. He was wearing a dark suit, a white tie, and had a white handkerchief in his pocket. Can you find him?

# TOWN-SQUARE MYSTERY

Sergeant Molinson raced across the town square with Trixie and Honey hard on his heels. "Tell me again about the robbery," he hollered over his shoulder.

"We were all in the club's station wagon," Trixie said breathlessly. "We were just passing Mr. Rozack's gas station when we saw someone holding him up. Whoever it was was wearing a mask."

Honey added, "The robber ran away. We followed him, and now the other Bob-Whites have him trapped inside the church on the corner."

Sergeant Molinson looked surprised. "The thief ran into the church?"

"Yes. That one," Trixie said, pointing.

In another moment, the police sergeant's feet pounded through the church's front door. He stopped, bewildered. A Bob-White was standing guard at every exit. Seated in the front pew were three angry people.

"Okay," the sergeant demanded, "which one is the thief?"

Brian frowned. "We aren't sure," he said. "These three people were all here in the church when we came in."

A young man rose to his feet. "This is an outrage!" he cried. "We've been herded in here like cattle! Even Moses treated his animals on the Ark better than this! I'm a Bible student, not a thief!"

"I agree!" an older man snarled. He was wearing grease-stained overalls. "I've been upstairs for the last hour cleaning the pipe organ. I didn't see or hear anything."

"Me, neither," a gray-haired woman announced angrily. "I was busy in a back room stitching new choir robes. I know nothing about a holdup, and I insist that you release us at once!"

"Sergeant Molinson," Trixie said, "the thief has given himself away."

The policeman agreed and took the thief into custody.

Which one was the thief?

# CRYPTIC LISTS

Each of the following lists of related words is in code.
Every letter stands for another letter. Each list has its
own code. Crack the codes and decipher the cryptic
words. We've given a "clue" to the first code.

## A

These words all have something to do with mysteries.

Example: detective

```
   c l u e
1. V D K R
```

```
      e
2. J Y I R O M J N Z M J W Y
```

```
     l  c e
3. U W D J V R
```

```
    l e u
4. O D R K M L
```

```
    e    e  ce
5.  R I J T R Y V R
```

```
      e c
6. J Y O U R V M W Q
```

```
   .c        l
7. V Q J B J Y Z D
```

```
    u    e c
8. O K O U R V M
```

## B

Here are some subjects that
Trixie and her friends study
in school.

Example: French

1. V M T O R H S

2. S R H G L I B

3. Z O T V Y I Z

4. Z I G

5. Y R L O L T B

6. X S V N R H G I B

7. K S B H R X H

8. H K Z M R H S

114

## C

Here are some sports and outdoor activities the Bob-Whites enjoy.

Example: horseback riding

1. KJBTNCKJUU

2. BJRURWP

3. LJVERWP

4. CNWWRB

5. LAXBB-LXDWCAH
   BTRRWP

6. BFRVVRWP

7. RLN BTJCRWP

8. KRLHLURWP

## D

All of the Bob-Whites have big appetites. Here are some foods they like to eat.

Example: pizza

1. GARMGMLLX HUM

2. SECGRLQMLN

3. OLMDIS OLUMN

4. CUAY NSEYMN

5. HMEDRP-GRPPML
   NEDKVUISMN

6. OLUMK ISUIYMD

7. ISFIFAEPM IEYM

8. HEDIEYMN

---

# QUICKIE QUIZ #3

Monopoly is a favorite board game of the Beldens and their friends. Do you like it, too? Can you name the four railroads in the game? Where are they on the board? How many "Chance" and "Community Chest" spaces are there? What space is directly kitty-corner to "GO"? What drawing appears in the "GO" space?

# MASQUERADE MYSTERY

1. IT SURE WAS NICE OF MR. PERKINS TO INVITE US TO HIS MASQUERADE PARTY.

2. SOME OF THESE COSTUMES ARE REALLY CLEVER! I'M GLAD WE COULD COME AS LOOK-ALIKES, THOUGH, IN OUR CLUB JACKETS.

3. RAY! CALL THE POLICE! SOMEONE BROKE INTO OUR SAFE UPSTAIRS!

**WHOM DOES TRIXIE SUSPECT?**

# STABLE
# TROUBLE

Trixie frowned as she hurried toward the Wheelers' stable. Someone was shouting—and it sounded like Regan!

A tearful Honey ran to meet her. "Trixie!" she cried. "Thank heavens you're here. While Regan was away on an errand, one of our houseguests, Paula Ratner, says she was injured by Jupiter! We know she's lying, but she says she's going to sue my father for every penny he has!"

A moment later, Trixie gasped at the sight that met her eyes. Jupiter, the Wheelers' beautiful jet black gelding, stood trembling outside his stall. His head drooped, his sides heaved, and his once-shining coat was streaked with dust and sweat. Someone had ridden him long and hard.

Regan was furious. "You may be a guest," he was yelling at the haughty-looking young woman, "but you should listen to what you're told! I said you could ride any horse *except* Jupiter. He's always been hard to handle, and I told you to stay completely away from him!"

"That's your story," sneered Paula Ratner. Her clothes were covered with mud, and her right foot was bruised and swelling fast. "*My* story is that you *recommended* that I take that black brute for a gallop across the fields!"

"That's not true!" Regan shouted at her.

Paula Ratner smirked. "I'll tell the judge that as soon as I'd put my foot in the stirrup to mount him, he took off like a bolt of lightning. My foot was caught and twisted badly. Why, I still don't know how I got free. It's a wonder I wasn't killed!"

"Oh, Trixie," Honey moaned. "What on earth can we do?"

"*I* know what you can do," Paula Ratner said. "You can tell your father to pay me damages now and save court costs!"

Trixie sighed. "No, Miss Ratner," she said. "You won't be getting a penny. You've injured your foot somehow, but not in the way you've just explained. Your story's false, and I can prove it!"

How could Trixie prove that Paula Ratner was lying?

# MYSTERY OF THE 13 SPACES

NOTE: This is a special quiz for readers of TRIXIE
BELDEN mysteries.

The locations pinpointed on the map below have been the
scenes of many Bob-White adventures. When you solve the
Mystery of the Thirteen Spaces, you will find the name of a
place that draws Trixie Belden like a magnet, a place she
just can't seem to stay away from.

The number beneath each blank space corresponds to
the number of the clue-question on the next page. The
answer to each question will be a location on the map.
Each location is labeled with a letter. That letter is to be
inserted in the blank space whose number corresponds to
the clue you've just solved. Some letters are used more than
once.

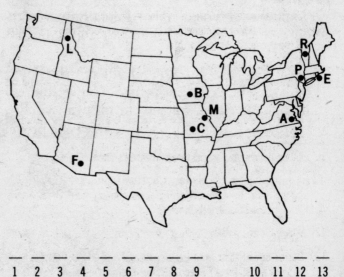

—  —  —  —  —  —  —  —  —      —  —  —  —
1   2   3   4   5   6   7   8   9      10  11  12  13

1. Trixie was saved from an attacking wildcat by a gunshot that seemed to come from nowhere—and her rescuer mysteriously vanished without a trace! Where did this happen?

2. Buried under tons of snow in an avalanche, Mart faced almost certain death. Where were the Bob-Whites on this occasion?

3. Trixie found a clue to a hundred-and-fifty-year-old mystery in the burial vault of a cemetery on the grounds of an antebellum mansion. Where was this mansion located?

4. Where did Jim, Brian, Mart—and Trixie—put on an impromptu basketball exhibition?

5. In the course of her investigations into a mystery, Trixie discovered that the Belden house had once been used as a "station" in the Underground Railroad in Civil War times. Where did this mystery eventually lead the Bob-Whites?

6. Where did Trixie find a German bank note that led to a mystery involving a gang of counterfeiters?

7. During a mystery involving a missing person and stolen art treasures, Trixie and Honey encountered a phantom on horseback—a phantom without a head! Where was this?

8. On a wilderness camping expedition, a Belden cousin disappeared, apparently the victim of an attack by a legendary beast. Where did this happen?

9. Trixie found a treasure map in an old bottle under the floorboards of a dilapidated gazebo. Where was this gazebo?

10. Where did the Bob-Whites finally meet Di's **real** Uncle Monty?

11. A search that began with an old letter found in the Belden attic ended with the discovery of a priceless family heirloom necklace. Where were these jewels hidden?

12. Where did the Bob-Whites first learn to cross-country ski?

13. During one of their most exciting adventures, the Bob-Whites were held for questioning by Secret Service agents. Where was this?

# ANSWERS

## Page 9, WHAT DO YOU KNOW ABOUT FIGHTING CRIME?

1.true 2.true 3.government 4.no 5.yes (by spraying it with shellac and dusting with talcum powder before pouring in the plaster) 6.fingerprints 7.false (It records body changes—such as blood pressure—as well as reflexes, all of which must be diagnosed.) 8.an international crime-fighting organization to which over 115 countries belong 9.France 10.to remain silent; to have an attorney present during questioning; to know that whatever he says may be used against him in court.

## Page 10, THE CASE OF THE DOMINANT DAME

Gorgeous Gladys.

## Page 10, THE CASE OF THE UNCERTAIN SEATING

Jim is driving, with Trixie next to him and Honey to Trixie's right. Mart is sitting directly behind Jim, with Di in the middle and Brian to her right.

## Page 11, MUSICAL MYSTERY

In each ad, they found the words that began with the same letters as the notes in the musical sequence. The first notes were *g f b g c d a*, and the day's message read: "Got First Bank's goods. Can deliver anytime." The notes were *c f a a f d f a f*, when the crook's partner answered the next day: "Corner (of) Fifth Avenue and Fair Drive, Friday at four."

## Pages 12–13, REDHEADED THIEF

If Larry's story were true, Aunt Mary's clock would have chimed only four times. California time is three hours behind that of New York State.

## Pages 14–15, THE KIDNAPPED CAMPER

The man said that when Harry was kidnapped, they were both asleep. He also said that he'd done nothing before he ran for help. Yet both sleeping bags were rolled up! (See panels 4 and 6.) When confronted with the evidence, the man confessed that he himself had kidnapped Harry in an effort to get money for his gambling debts. Harry was rescued a short time later.

## Pages 16–17, PIRATES AND PIRATE TREASURE

1.a 2.a 3.true (although there are doubts as to how much the pirates actually buried) 4.neither (A doubloon is an old Spanish gold coin.) 5.A red flag signaled that no mercy would be given. 6.c (Many have searched for the treasure off the Costa Rica coast.) 7.*Treasure Island* 8.Sir Francis Drake 9.Anne Bonney and Mary Read—women disguised as men! 10.a—pyramid; the extended side points in the direction of the treasure b—cross; the longest arm points in the direction of the treasure c—wiggling snake; the head points in the direction of the treasure d—stairs; the treasure is down the stairs e—treasure chest f—bag of treasure g—turtle; this sign means danger h—cave or tunnel i—river or stream to be crossed j—mark meaning that the treasure was directly below k—coiled snake; the head pointing to the treasure below l—sun; the treasure was very close to, or under, this mark.

## Pages 18–19, RODEO CLOWN

Bulls are attracted to movement, not color. Bulls are color blind. Also, a real cowboy would not refer to himself as a *bullfighter*. Hank was really just a college student from the city trying to earn some extra money. Thanks to Trixie's quick thinking, he was kept out of the ring and saved from possible serious injury.

## Page 20, LOST LETTERS

1.Seattle, Washington 2.Milwaukee, Wisconsin 3.Denver, Colorado 4.Pittsburgh, Pennsylvania 5.Phoenix, Arizona 6.Atlanta, Georgia.

## Page 20, HARDHEADS AND SUCKERS

Jim's note contained a list of fish! All of the fish come from the Hudson River (near which Trixie and her friends live), and she needed to learn about them for her biology class.

## Page 21, INSCRUTABLE BEDTIME STORIES

1.Little Red Riding Hood 2.Jack and the Beanstalk 3.Goldilocks and the Three Bears 4.Hansel and Gretel 5.The Three Little Pigs.

## Pages 22-23, THE SUSPICIOUS PROFESSOR

If no one had been in the lab for a week, all of the water ($H_2O$) in the open beaker (see panel 5) would have evaporated.

## Pages 24-25, LONG-LOST GRANDSON

Australia lies south of the equator; therefore, New Year's Day would be in the middle of summer there, not winter. Furthermore, the man would have had to have identification in order to enter the United States!

## Pages 26-27, BATTER UP!

1.b 2.b 3.a 4.a 5.d 6.d 7.c 8.b 9.c 10.c.

## Page 27, QUICKIE QUIZ #1

The names of the reindeer are Dasher, Dancer, Prancer, Vixen, Comet, Cupid, Donner, Blitzen. The author was Clement C. Moore, and he titled his poem *A Visit From St. Nicholas.*

## Page 28, BAFFLERS

1.Neil A. Armstrong landed on the moon. 2.an antique Ford ("Tin Lizzie") 3.balloon, first Atlantic crossing.

## Page 29, COUNTERFEIT ART

In the counterfeit drawing, the horse has no saddle, and her markings are different. The rider is missing her gloves; she carries her crop at a different angle;

and part of her hairbow is missing. The dog has only three legs. The bush at right bends the opposite way, the slant of the hill is different, and the sun has been added to the sky. The artist's signature is omitted.

### Pages 30–31, LITTLE BOYS GONE!

The three little boys were inside the house. The deep, rounded *toe* marks told Trixie the whole story. The boys went to the paddock before it snowed and returned home afterward—walking backward! Trixie found them right where she expected their out-in-the-snow appetites would take them—in the kitchen, eating huge pieces of coffee cake, still warm from the oven.

### Page 32, LOSERS—AND WINNERS

1.a 2.b (An average eight-year-old boy weighs sixty to seventy pounds!) 3.Yes 4.b 5.He heard that the rest of the horses were no longer in the race; all had fallen or been disqualified—except his.

### Page 33, WHAT A STATE!

1.Ark. 2.Mass. 3.Tenn. 4.Ore. 5.Md. 6.Pa. 7.Wash. 8.Miss. 9.Ill. 10.Me.

### Pages 34–35, THE MISSING FOOTPRINTS

The teakettle gave the owner away. He said he'd put it on the fire an hour before, but it didn't boil, even though the flame was fairly high (see panels 4 and 6), until he was talking to Sergeant Molinson. The owner had staged the robbery in order to collect the insurance, but he'd been foiled by an alert Trixie Belden. Trixie and Mart took their mother's watch to another jeweler for repair.

## Pages 36–37, DINING-ROOM THIEF

Bob, the busboy, was the thief. Ice takes up more space than liquid water; therefore, the water glasses could not have overflowed from the melting ice. Bob, then, had too much unexplained time in which to steal the handbag. When Trixie successfully challenged his alibi, he confessed, and the purse was returned to Mrs. Boyer.

## Page 38, MISSING PARTNERS

1.bolts 2.Bailey 3.stripes 4.Minnie 5.Marie 6.Ernie 7.the lion 8.Dale 9.paper 10.sea 11.rider 12.tell 13.shine 14.eggs 15.downs 16.relaxation 17.tell 18.large 19.around 20.honey 21.there 22.shake 23.Edith 24.go 25.lightning 26.reap 27.write 28.socket 29.board 30.blues 31.Gretel 32.death 33.comb 34.carriage 35.water 36.nail.

## Pages 39–40, DI'S MEMORY SHARPENER

1.goose, grasshopper 2.thermometer, wristwatch, envelope 3.ski 4.radio 5.flowerpot 6.saddle, glove, skateboard, ski, broom (if you're a witch) 7.envelope, broom 8.sprinkling can 9.ski, radio (CB—snowmobiling et al.), saddle, football, skateboard, broom (cricket, curling), glove 10.locket 11.lemon 12.stepladder 13.skateboard 14.grasshopper 15.envelope, locket 16.violin 17.candle 18.earmuffs 19.radio, wristwatch 20.goose

## Page 41, TRIXIE'S HIDDEN-ANSWER QUIZ

1.*c* (The igloo melts.) 2.*r* (The radio communicates by sound, the rest by sight.) 3.*a* (It is a wild dog; the others are vessels.) 4.*n* (the only one that flies) 5.*e* (It is a color; the others are numbers.) The bird world's "champion weight lifter": *crane.*

## Page 41, QUIZ FOR COGITATORS

Trixie's classmate spoke soon after the New Year. She had been thirteen all the previous year until her birthday on December 29, when she turned fourteen. This year, she will be fifteen on December 29, and next year, she will be sixteen on that date!

## Pages 42–43, POOR LOSER

If Bernie had stopped immediately when he felt the impact, as he claimed he had, the bike would have been crushed under his *front* wheels. Bernie confessed and bought Dave Andersen a new bike.

## Page 44, HELP!

1.h 2.c 3.e 4.d 5.g 6.f 7.b 8.a.

## Page 45, ANIMALS—STORYBOOK AND OTHERWISE

1.the Cheshire Cat in *Alice in Wonderland* 2.Cowardly Lion in *The Wonderful Wizard of Oz* 3.the

Trojan Horse 4.Mickey Mouse 5.Elsa, the lioness 6.the Cow Who Jumped Over the Moon 7.Lassie 8.Rudolph, the Red-Nosed Reindeer 9.Smokey the Bear 10.Pegasus.

## Pages 46–47, THE STOLEN HORSE

Trixie knew that furniture vans don't deliver on Sunday (note calendar in panel 2—Di was going on her trip the next day). Trixie further reasoned that the furniture van was the only thing that had gone by that was big enough to hold a horse. That the van had "motor trouble" so near Sunny's stable increased Trixie's suspicions. Sure enough, when Sergeant Molinson located the van a few minutes later, Di's handsome palomino was found inside it, safe and sound.

## Pages 48–49, THE FIRE

Trixie waited until the electricity came back on, then turned on Mrs. Pritchard's air conditioner. She knew that old air conditioners make lots of noise—so that no one could possibly have heard a small boy run past.

## Page 50, ABOUT HORSES

1.polo 2.Arabian 3.no (Some can be found on the Mongolian plains in Asia.) 4.donkeys, zebras 5.one 6.b 7.no (The palomino is not a breed at all; any golden horse is a palomino.) 8.Tennessee Walking Horse 9.Belgian 10.Thoroughbred.

### Page 51, SODA-POP MIX-UP

orange.

### Page 80, REGAN'S HELPER?

The third horse picture, the lampshade, the horse trophy, and the rug are all upside down. The footstool is on its side. The andirons are *inside* the fireplace. The clock is facing the wall. The television antenna and the middle sofa cushion didn't get put back at all.

### Page 81, FAMOUS PLACES IN THE UNITED STATES

1.St. Louis 2.Alcatraz 3.Alamo 4.Washington, D.C. 5.New York 6.San Francisco 7.the Statue of Liberty 8.Plymouth 9.Sutter's Mill 10.Philadelphia.

### Pages 82–83, THE SUSPECT IN THE RESTAURANT

Trixie was suspicious because he lied about being there over an hour—his coat was still dripping! (See panel 7.)

### Pages 84–85, THE MONEY JAR

The electric clock was accurate, so Trixie knew that somebody had set it during the night after the storm had passed and the electricity was restored. Hot-tempered Steve Simpson wouldn't have thought of this, but precise, punctual Gary Slade would automatically have done it. When the police searched

Slade's apartment (with a warrant), they found the money jar, and Slade confessed.

## Pages 86–87, DOODLERS' NOODLERS

1.time-out 2.cross-country 3.hit the pocket 4.tee off 5.butterfly 6.triple play 7.touch line 8.left end 9.long horse 10.foul (fowl) ball 11.double dribble 12.hang ten.

## Page 88, CRYPTO-TRIXIE

Trixie was right, and her next step was to ask Sergeant Molinson to notify the FBI. Here's why: The message was a cryptogram in which the sequence of the letters of the alphabet was in reverse—Z was substituted for A, Y was substituted for B, and so forth. "Miss Lovely's" real message was:

> Dear Joey, You idiot! The FBI has caught on that I'm using my newspaper office as a front for illegal zither-smuggling. Thanks to you, I am now on their ten-most-wanted list—as a man! It's going to be hard for me to keep disguising myself as Miss Lovely much longer. Quick!—arrange for X rays and plastic surgery at St. Mary's immediately. I want to be made handsome enough to become headwaiter at La Gourmet Restaurant. Right now I'm too ugly to even wash their dishes!

## Page 89, THE CASE OF THE SEMICIRCULAR SUSPECTS

Freddy the Fink.

## Page 89, THE CASE OF
## THE PHANTOM SHOPLIFTER

Artful Arlene.

## Pages 90–91, THE HOLDUP

No self-respecting painter has shoes that are anything but paint-daubed, yet this man wore polished black oxfords. He had run from the supermarket into the church, put paint-stained coveralls on over his clothes, then tried to walk away undetected.

## Pages 92–93, THE EXCHANGE STUDENT

The window was down, and there were several moths fluttering around the bedroom lamp (see panel 4), but not in the rest of the house.

## Pages 94–95, LEGENDS AND FOLKLORE

1.a 2.d.

## Pages 96–97, THE SHOPPER

Trixie knew that the woman didn't need glasses to read the price tag; she had just read a newspaper item in the shop window. When the woman stopped Mrs. Wheeler, therefore, Trixie was alerted. She was sure she saw the woman's hand go into Mrs. Wheeler's bag, then transfer something to her own bag. Trixie proved this when she fell, taking the woman's bag with her. The thief escaped from the shop, but she had to abandon her stolen property, and the police were able to return the wallets to other victims of the pickpocket and the necklace to the store.

## Page 98, WORD LADDERS

(Note: Other answers are possible.)

| CODE | WILD | FOOT | SONG | SLOW |
|------|------|------|------|------|
| CORE | WILE | BOOT | SANG | SLOT |
| CORD | TILE | BOLT | SAND | SOOT |
| WORD | TIME | BOLL | BAND | LOOT |
|      | TAME | BALL | BIND | LOST |
|      |      |      | BIRD | LAST |
|      |      |      |      | FAST |

## Page 99, THE MYSTERIOUS MAP

Trixie realized that the map was of her own neighborhood and that the arrow on it was pointing to the Bob-White clubhouse. Then she began at Y and read every other letter, going around the map clockwise, then counterclockwise. The card read: "You are invited to a surprise party for Mart at the clubhouse now."

## Pages 100–101, FOR SUPERSTITIOUS FOLK ONLY

1.so money will soon fill your pocket 2.a letter or a present—to arrive when the white spot reaches the tip 3.because what you are thinking might come true (That's why some people are careful to think only good thoughts when they feel a sneeze coming.) 4.Put it in your shoe. 5.Cut a thin slice from the stalk end—

if you see a Y-shaped spot, your wish should come true. 6.because you must wish before the star is out of sight 7.because they are supposed to be luckier than others 8.They will be well all summer. 9.Run around a four-legged object, such as a chair or a dog, three times—or decide not to be superstitious (and what fun is *that!*). 10.The first two and the last four should bring good luck; all the rest, bad luck.

### Page 101, QUICKIE QUIZ #2

Huey, Dewey, and Louie belong to the Junior Wood-chucks; April, May, and June are Chickadees.

### Pages 102–103, THE EXTERMINATORS

The man carried the "snake" in a burlap sack, and he held the sack with his bare hand. Had the snake been real, it could easily have struck at him through the burlap. Trixie knew no real exterminator would be so careless. The police arrived while the con men were still in the basement, and they discovered that the "snake" in the sack was only a toy noisemaker. The "exterminators" went to jail. Of course, there hadn't been any snakes in Mrs. Turner's basement.

### Pages 104–105, STOP, THIEF!

The man's apron was much too long (see panel 5) for him to be the real butcher. And he was perspiring too much (see panels 6 and 7) to have just been in a cold meat locker. Trixie rightly guessed that when he saw the police, he had pushed the real owner of the store into the meat locker, then tried to divert attention from himself with his story.

## Pages 106–107, EXPLORING CAVES

1.She is a stone figure formed by the constant dripping of water on rock for many centuries. 2.spelunker 3.a 4.c 5.the oldest-known manuscripts of any books of the Bible, including almost all of the Old Testament 6.yes (tapir and peccary) 7.false—only in the past century or so 8.a 9.true (For example, the reaction of mind and body to a feeling of timelessness is similar in both outer space and inner depths.) 10.true 11.true 12.true 13.alone, light, strength 14.Stalactites hang from the ceiling; stalagmites form on the ground. 15.countless thousands of bats.

## Pages 108–109, THE NEPHEW

The senior citizens' magazine did not mention Mrs. Forsythe's maiden name, Soames. Since she had been a small child when her brother left home, and since that brother never returned, it was highly unlikely that the brother's son could have known that Mrs. Forsythe of Sleepyside had once been Evalina Soames of Albany. Trixie's suspicions proved correct. Mrs. Forsythe's "nephew" turned out to be a confidence man who learned what he could about elderly widows—such as their maiden name and what family they had—then made their acquaintance and persuaded them to draw money out of the bank to invest in phony mining stocks.

## Page 110, TRIXIE AND HONEY'S REVENGE

1.b ("The sky is falling.") 2.a ("There's a sucker born every minute.") 3.j ("What a good boy am I.") 4.e ("Go West, young man, go West.") 5.g ("Let them eat cake.") 6.f ("I'll blow your house down.") 7.i ("One small step for a man . . .") 8.c ("Ask not what your country can do for you . . .") 9.h ("If you can't stand the heat, stay out of the kitchen.") 10.d ("Old soldiers never die.")

## Page 111, EMBEZZLER!

The embezzler is the third man from the left.

## Pages 112–113, TOWN-SQUARE MYSTERY

Any Bible student would know that it was Noah, not Moses, who boarded the Ark. Sergeant Molinson found the stolen money in the young "Bible student's" pocket.

## Pages 114–115, CRYPTIC LISTS

| A | B |
|---|---|
| 1. clue | 1. English |
| 2. investigation | 2. history |
| 3. police | 3. algebra |
| 4. sleuth | 4. art |
| 5. evidence | 5. biology |
| 6. inspector | 6. chemistry |
| 7. criminal | 7. physics |
| 8. suspect | 8. Spanish |

| C | D |
|---|---|
| 1. basketball | 1. blueberry pie |
| 2. sailing | 2. hamburgers |
| 3. camping | 3. french fries |
| 4. tennis | 4. milk shakes |
| 5. cross-country skiing | 5. peanut-butter sandwiches |
| 6. swimming | 6. fried chicken |
| 7. ice skating | 7. chocolate cake |
| 8. bicycling | 8. pancakes |

## Page 115, QUICKIE QUIZ #3

The four railroads are the Reading, Pennsylvania, B&O, and Short Line; each one is in the middle of a side. There are three "Chance" and three "Community Chest" spaces. "FREE PARKING" is kitty-corner from "GO," which has an arrow pictured on it.

## Pages 116–117, MASQUERADE MYSTERY

Trixie realized that one of the guests must have made the strange tracks (see panel 5). She deduced that the footprints were indistinct because they were not made by a regular shoe and that the line between them was made by something dragging. When the police came, Trixie directed them to the only one who fit this description: the woman in the leopard costume.

## Pages 118–119, STABLE TROUBLE

Paula Ratner's *right* foot was bruised and swollen. A horse is mounted from the left side with the *left* foot.

1.*C* (Missouri Ozarks) 2.*R* (Vermont) 3.*A* (Virginia) 4.*B* (Iowa) 5.*A* (Virginia) 6.*P* (Sleepyside) 7.*P* (Sleepyside) 8.*L* (Idaho) 9.*E* (Cobbett's Island) 10.*F* (Arizona) 11.*A* (Virginia) 12.*R* (Vermont) 13.*M* (St. Louis). Trixie loves to be at home on *CRABAPPLE FARM*.